REAL TIME

A NOVEL

by Pnina Moed Kass

CLARION BOOKS/NEW YORK

This book is a work of fiction. Any references to historical events, real people, or real locales are used fictitiously. Other names, characters, places, and incidents are products of the author's imagination, and any resemblance to actual events or locales or to persons, living or dead, is entirely coincidental.

Clarion Books
a Houghton Mifflin Company imprint
215 Park Avenue South, New York, NY 10003
Copyright © 2004 by Pnina Moed Kass

Excerpt from "Dry Loaf," from *The Collected Poems of Wallace Stevens,*
reprinted by permission of Random House, Inc.

The text was set in 11-point Sabon.

www.houghtonmifflinbooks.com

Printed in the U.S.A.

Library of Congress Cataloging-in-Publication Data
Kass, Pnina.
Real time / by Pnina Moed Kass.
p.   cm.
Summary: Sixteen-year-old Thomas Wanninger persuades his mother to let him leave Germany to volunteer at a kibbutz in Israel, where he experiences a violent political attack and finds answers about his own past.
ISBN 0-618-44203-0
1. Germans—Israel—Juvenile fiction. [1. Germans—Israel—Fiction. 2. Terrorism—Fiction. 3. Interpersonal relations—Fiction. 4. Family—Fiction. 5. Israel—Fiction.] I. Title.
PZ7.K15443Re   2004
[Fic]—dc22   2004008481

ISBN-13: 978-0-618-44203-4
ISBN-10: 0-618-44203-0

QUM   10 9 8 7 6 5 4 3 2 1

To B. A. Moskowitz, author and critic,
editor and reader,
a friend like no other

ACKNOWLEDGMENTS

Many people, in many ways, helped me. For medical information and hospital procedures, thanks to Prof. Charles Weissman, Ron Krumer, Meital Ribowski, and Audrey Shimron at Hadassah, Israel, and Marcie Natan at Hadassah, U.S.A. Invaluable medical input was provided by Joe Rybicki, C.R.N.A., his wife, Heidi, and Naomi Hoffman, R.N. My thanks to Yad Vashem for their assistance. Time given to me by Reina Nuernberger, American International School, Kfar Shmaryahu, Israel, was much appreciated. Thanks to Samuel Melcer and Harry Adler for their German and Spanish. Gratitude to my agents, Deborah Harris in Israel and Nancy Gallt in the United States. My heartfelt thanks to Dinah Stevenson at Clarion Books for incisive editing and generosity of spirit.

It is equal to living in a tragic land
To live in a tragic time.

—Wallace Stevens, "Dry Loaf"

SUNDAY, APRIL 9

Thomas Wanninger Departure terminal, Schonefeld Airport   4:45 AM
(SXF), Berlin

"Thomas Wanninger?"

"Yes."

"Traveling alone?"

"Yes."

"First trip to Israel?"

"Yes."

"Passport, please."

I hand it over.

He opens it. He looks at the passport photo, looks at me, looks at the photo. "Born in Germany?"

"Yes."

"What is the purpose of your visit?"

"I'll be a volunteer at a kibbutz."

"Which kibbutz?"

"Broshim. It's outside Jerusalem."

"Can you show me proof of that?"

I unzip my backpack and stick my hand in. I can feel the sports magazine, the guidebook. I look sideways inside—there's a pack of tissues, some stuff from school I'm supposed to read, chewing gum . . . junk . . . junk . . . where did I put the letter from the kibbutz? I see him watching me as if I'm

3

some kind of suspect. Suddenly I think—he's not going to let me on the plane.

"Maybe you should empty your backpack, Thomas?"

I slide the backpack off my shoulder and squat on the ground.

He isn't taking his eyes off me for a minute. Another guy comes over, looks at me, and then whispers something into his ear. He nods and shows this guy my passport and airplane ticket. The guy walks away. My T-shirt is stuck to my armpits. Everything is on the floor. Then I see the pale blue information booklet and the letter is sticking out of it.

"Here it is." I hand it to him. I'm still squatting, waiting.

He looks at it, reads it. "Okay, put your stuff back in."

I jam everything into the backpack and stand up.

"Who packed your suitcase?"

"I did."

"Did anyone give you a gift or a package or any item to deliver when you arrive?"

"No."

"You're sure about that?"

"Yes."

"Do you have any relatives in Israel?"

"No—I'm not Jewish." I want him to believe me.

He looks at me like he doesn't. "For your information, there are non-Jews living in Israel. There are Christians, Muslims, Greek Orthodox, Druse—do you want me to continue?" He doesn't wait for my answer.

He looks at me, lifts the suitcase, turns it around, sees the yellow security sticker, puts it down. "Do you speak Arabic?"

"Arabic? No, of course I don't know Arabic!"

"All right. I'm just asking."

"Well, I don't know Arabic and I don't know Hebrew. I speak German, like we're talking now, right? And English." By now I'm sure I'm not going anywhere. In an hour I'll probably be back home. The people in line behind me are staring at me. Like I have a rash, like they're going to catch something from me. No one's missing a single one of his questions or my answers.

And then suddenly he hands back my passport, my ticket, and the kibbutz letter. Doesn't smile, just says, "Okay, you can go." It's over. He starts questioning the person in line behind me. Whatever he thought of me, of my passport, of what I looked like, it's history now. I can get on the plane.

Thomas Wanninger El Al flight 01: SXF–TLV (Berlin–Tel Aviv) 5:30 AM

The seat belt sign blinks red, the engines start to roar, the plane begins to taxi. The flight attendants are walking down the aisle, chatting with passengers, adjusting overhead bins, checking seat belts. Somewhere in the front of the plane a baby is squealing and then beginning to cry. I see the mother start to get up, but the flight attendant points to the lit seat belt sign. She sits down again.

I'm watching and listening to everything, I'm hyped up. Everything around me looks like it's in fluorescent light, and sounds are funneling through me on high volume. I'm going to a place I don't know, to find out something that no one at home knows, and if anyone thinks I'm calm, they're wrong.

I've flown only once before, on a school ski trip. But it isn't the same this time, I'll be entering a war zone. And I'm alone. There are flight announcements about the altitude of the plane, the weather, and perfume and cigarettes that will be sold duty-free. Maybe I'll buy perfume for Mutti—something in a pretty bottle. Then the pilot announces the estimated time of arrival.

The plane reaches the end of the runway and lifts off, tilting away from the ground slowly with almost no angle. It's six o'clock in the morning. Four more hours and I'll land in Israel. The announcement continues: "Local Israeli time is one hour ahead." I change the time on my watch. I've left German time behind. I have the whole row to myself. I stretch my legs and stare out the window.

The plane is cruising over the city. Berlin is concealed behind a thin veil of rain. Through the morning darkness I can see the dots of highway lights and the snaking line of traffic. Mutti must be in her car, driving in one of those lanes leading away from the airport. She probably won't go back home—she hates an empty house. If I know my mother, she'll go to the office, or travel to one of the branches of Hanseatic Insurance, or schedule a meeting with her boss. Mutti has to be busy. She says, "When I work, I forget."

The plane starts a steep climb, moves through clusters of clouds, and then pulls out into clear sky. Past my own reflection in the window it's all blue air, the color of early morning. Beyond the wing the blue is beginning to lighten. Somewhere the morning has started. It will be late morning when I arrive. The engines become a monotonous drone.

I unzip my backpack and take out the pamphlet. I don't bother unfolding it. I've read it and stared at the pictures a hundred times. The green rolling Judean Hills, the distant outlines of Jerusalem, the orderly row of red-roofed kibbutz houses, the auditorium, the guest hostel where I'll be staying. To myself, and only to myself, I am willing to admit I'm scared out of my mind. Not to Mutti, not to Rudi, even though he's my best buddy, and certainly not to Christina.

The time off from school wasn't tough to get. The principal is really hot on us going to Israel. *No generation of Germans should forget* is his motto. The real reason I'm going is my business. And I can't be a coward.

So here I am, about to land in a country where bombs go off every five seconds. Why am I doing this? Because I'm looking for information about a Nazi.

My grandfather.

One more time I read the letter I showed the security guy:

Shalom, Thomas!

Welcome to the SEEK program (See-Explore-Educate-Know) at Kibbutz Broshim, located outside Jerusalem. Our mailing address is Kibbutz Broshim, Doar Na 832, Jerusalem, Israel. Since you indicated an interest in agricultural work, we have arranged for you to work in the hothouses and plant nursery. Kibbutz Broshim exports flowers, and your help will be greatly appreciated. You will be instructed by Baruch Ben Tov, a very experienced gardener.

I reread the instructions for what I'm supposed to do when I land, though I know them by heart:

After landing and passing through Passport Control, look for someone holding a "SEEK" sign. This will be Vera Brodsky, who lives at Kibbutz Broshim and will be your "buddy" during your stay. Vera will be waiting for you inside the arrivals terminal of the airport. In case of any change, call 02-555-3242.

I shift around in the seat and feel the bulge in the back pocket of my jeans. The airplane ticket and passport—I forgot to put them back in the zippered pouch of my backpack. That's all I need, to lose my ticket and passport. The passport is dark red, with a stiff cover and a gold embossed eagle in the center. Printed underneath the eagle emblem, in big letters, is BUNDESREPUBLIK DEUTSCHLAND. I run my fingers over the spread wings. Eagles are birds of prey, aren't they? Why does a German passport have an eagle on the cover? Was my grandfather a bird of prey, waiting to lunge and capture, maybe to kill?

I flip open my passport to the inside page:

FAMILIEN NAME	*Wanninger*
NAME	*Thomas*
STAATSANHÖRIGKEIT	*Deutsch*
GEBURTSTORT	*Berlin*

The photo at the left of the typed information is me: unsmiling, brown eyes opened wide by the flash of the camera, short hair, and part of a white T-shirt. A high school kid who looks older than sixteen—at least that's what people tell me.

6:30 AM **Interrogation room, police headquarters, Jerusalem**

POLICE OFFICER: You understand you're not under arrest, don't you?

OMAR JOULANI: If you say so.

POLICE OFFICER: Of course we say so. Why would we lie? We just want information. You live in the same village as Sameh Laham, right?

OMAR JOULANI: No, in Jabel Fahm. And you know it. You know everything. But we go to the same high school. When there's no curfew. It's our last year.

POLICE OFFICER: Why aren't you in school today?

OMAR JOULANI: How can I be in school if you brought me here? Anyway, I don't go to school. Instead I work. I study at night.

POLICE OFFICER: And Sameh? Does he also study at night?

OMAR JOULANI: I don't know what Sameh does. But I study. All night.

POLICE OFFICER: Do you study bomb making?

OMAR JOULANI: No, I study history. Who did what to whom, how the Jews keep the myth of the Holocaust going while they do genocide to us.

POLICE OFFICER: Congratulations, you probably got one hundred in history. So, getting back to your best friend. You don't know what he does . . . ?

OMAR JOULANI: I'm his friend, not his guard. That's your job. Me, I study and I work.

POLICE OFFICER: Good, that means you're a smart boy and a strong boy. You look strong, really strong.

OMAR JOULANI: I'm not that strong. I mean, I wouldn't be able to do anything—anything violent, that is.

POLICE OFFICER: So you're just into books, right? You never touch knives or guns, do you?

OMAR JOULANI: I don't touch them or see them. I swear by Allah. I start shaking, my whole body, when I even think of someone being hurt. And Sameh too, he wouldn't harm anyone. His Jewish boss loves him like a son, like his own son.

POLICE OFFICER: Oh, he has a Jewish boss. Now, that interests us. Where is this Jewish boss?

OMAR JOULANI: I don't know. It's illegal to hire us. Don't think I'm stupid.

POLICE OFFICER: So you don't know where the Jewish boss is, what his business is. Do you know where the bomb factory is? You know about bombs, don't you? Your buddy, Rashid, said you were the best student in chemistry class.

OMAR JOULANI: Rashid is a liar and a stinking little thief. You have him in jail, and he'll say anything.

POLICE OFFICER: He says you know how to explode bombs, Omar. He says you have a real touch with them. You get high as if you're on drugs when you make them.

OMAR JOULANI: You're trying to get me to say I'm one of those— a *shaheed*. I won't say it. I'm not. I sell vegetables with my grandfather.

POLICE OFFICER: Where is Sameh?

OMAR JOULANI: I told you, I don't know. Go to the Jewish man who is his boss.

POLICE OFFICER: We don't know who that is. No one ever heard of Sameh. So, Omar, it seems your best friend has disappeared. *Suspect looks at the floor and does not respond.*

POLICE OFFICER: Three days and no one knows where he is.

OMAR JOULANI: Sameh has a cousin in a village near Jerusalem. Maybe he went there.

POLICE OFFICER: What is the name of the village?

OMAR JOULANI: I can't remember.

POLICE OFFICER: Try. Try very hard.

OMAR JOULANI: Please let me go home. I'm sure Sameh will show up today. You'll see.

POLICE OFFICER: Why do you say that? Why are you so sure?

OMAR JOULANI: They are without food in his family. He must work.

POLICE OFFICER: We can keep you longer—you know that.

OMAR JOULANI: I know that. But I know nothing. Nothing. Please.

POLICE OFFICER: Release him.

6:30 AM Baruch Ben Tov Kibbutz Broshim, Judean Hills

The boy from Germany is coming today. His arrival throws me back into the past. He's not the first German student to come here, but he's the first who will work in the flower fields and hothouses. The first who will be under my supervision. Of course I was consulted. Will you mind working with a German boy, Baruch? I was asked. No, of course not, I answered. I am a member of the kibbutz and will do my share. But I am uneasy. What will this Thomas Wanninger say when he sees the number on my arm? Will he foolishly apologize? Will he speak to me in German? Does he know I speak German? It is an intrusion in my life. I will speak to him in English.

The sun has risen, warming the air and making the last of the night sky very light. I hear the birds speak to one another, the dew hangs transparent from each petal, the sprinklers whirr in the still spring air. I always walk up and down the rows of sunflowers at this hour. No one is here. I can say, "Rachel,

Ruchele," and no one hears me. Her name is my morning prayer.

Rachel was wonderful with her hands. She would have planted sunflowers and dahlias, petunias, daisies, everything. Even in the room under the roof she painted flowers on the enamel plates we ate from. Her hands were like the wind and her imagination endless. She turned the attic into our palace. What she would have made of this solitary place, this small house I live in!

And books—goodness, how she loved books. She would smile to see me now, not the professor of anthropology I wanted to be but a simple gardener. If she were here, she would lead me by the hand to my shelf of poetry books and she'd recite the poems of Goethe, the German poems we both learned in school. Remember, she'd certainly say, and laugh if I couldn't remember some lines or the teacher who taught us.

But she's not here. She was buried fifty feet from the wall that closed us in, surrounded us, in the old cemetery of the ghetto. The Germans bulldozed it, looking for tunnels. God only knows where her body is now.

All of us who hid in the attic that night had to run for our lives. I wrapped her body in the flowered down comforter, her and the baby together.

Vladek and I timed the German patrols, waiting for them to pass through our street. When we heard the steps of their heavy boots fade away, we dared to creep out of the attic and down the stairs.

We dug the grave in the muddy soil between the sewer pipes and the wall. There was almost no time to hold her and the baby, seconds only. No time to recite the words of *Kaddish,* the prayer for the dead. Only time enough for those six words I'd known since I was a child: *"Shema Yisrael, Adonai Eloheinu, Adonai Ehad."*

Thomas Wanninger will arrive this afternoon. I will be polite and considerate to him. After all, I have not lost my senses. He's a young man, he's not to blame for my past.

6:30 AM **Sameh Laham** Zebedeid, Palestinian Authority

When I've got my hands in the grease and food scraps of the stinking sink full of dishes, I talk to myself. This is what you will be doing when you're twenty-three, Sameh. And twenty-four. Forever, probably. You'll be washing the floor, scrubbing the marks left by soldiers' boots. Is this what you will be doing, Sameh? No, Sameh, you will not be doing this. You will do something brave and heroic. You will save your mother's life, and your sisters and your brothers will remember you forever.

I know the fields that lead back to the diner. I know them like the narrow streets of my village. I could be blindfolded and still find my way to Zebedeid, to the intersection, to Jerusalem. My mind is a map of bushes I can hide behind, gullies I can drop into, holes in the barbed wire I can squeeze through, boulders I can roll to cover a cave. I know all of these. I am the lord of this territory. It is mine, no one else's.

Omar is a pal of mine from school. He's from Jabel Fahm. He was the best soccer player in our class. Quick as a fox and eyes that saw all the moves on the field. I should have been born in Brazil, he always said—I would have been greater than Pelé. He said it so often we started to call him "Pelé."

Last month, when I came back home, zigzagging around the blockades, proud I'd fooled those little soldiers, he laughed at me. You want to be a hero, he said, listen to me. And he told me about his idea, an idea that would make me a hero.

It's almost seven. The Boss called Omar with a message: Tell Sameh he's still got his job if he comes back today. Today I'll go back to work.

> Thomas Wanninger, 16 years old, born and lives in
> Berlin. Father died of cancer, lives with mother, no
> brothers or sisters. High school student, majors in
> mathematics and physics. Wants to be an architect.
> Reason stated for joining SEEK program: "interested
> in learning about Israel."

Everybody has more than one reason for coming here, to this
country, and the same goes for the kibbutz. There's the *real* reason and then there's the reason you write down on the application. After all, you want the kibbutz to accept you, don't you?
And don't we all, at one time or another, say or write what we
know adults want to hear?

Take my friend Lidia, who's from Argentina. She showed me
a copy of her application. Her paragraph was full of stuff about
how all she wanted was to work and live on a farm. "I'll be
happy working in the cowsheds or the canning factory, or snap-
ping pictures of kibbutz events." Her *real* reason? To live in a
place where she wasn't going to be afraid. Her father passed
out pamphlets against the government in Argentina, along with
the eggs and milk he sold in his grocery store. The store was
closed down twice. She grew up when her country was under a
military dictatorship. Lidia said it was a miracle she didn't end
up in jail.

As for me, I wrote down on my application that I wanted to
study botany and live on a kibbutz. "My dream is to perfect
plants that need very little water and plants that can grow without chemical sprays." The kibbutz accepted me.

The *real* reason I'm here is that Sergei—my best friend, my
love—committed suicide. We had promised each other we'd go
to Israel and live together all our lives. He broke the promise. So
selfish, so very selfish.

13

Sergei, wherever you are, can you hear me? You ruined my life. You lied to me.

I still don't understand why someone would desert the person he loved. Without saying a word. Make me think it was my fault.

I came to Israel on my own. I dug my hands into the soil and made things grow, yes, even a small lilac bush to remind me of Odessa. Lilacs—you can go crazy with their smell. Full bursts of purple and lavender, a mist of perfume, a smell from home. I live in a place with endless fruit orchards and vineyards.

Without you, Sergei. You should have been here with me.

Now that I have Dan, I can't stop thinking—will I lose him, too? Can I trust him? Can he trust me?

It was Baruch Ben Tov, my guide and my teacher, who got me through the first months. He's a silent man but he's absolutely dependable, like a sign on a trail, immovable and always there, pointing you in the right direction.

After three years, he convinced the housing committee to give me my own place. No more sharing—I can't believe it. Lidia painted a sunflower on the door and wrote V-E-R-A on the petals. It's been a few months since I moved in, but even now when I open the door, I am thrilled—I get the chills: This is mine, all mine. I earned it working in the fields, doing kitchen duty, sorting laundry, everything everyone else does. The day I moved in, Baruch gave me a hug and a bouquet of white daisies and told me, "You look more and more like a farmer and less and less like a Bolshoi ballerina."

"I've never been so happy. The earth will never desert me; what I plant will grow. Even my lilacs, like in Odessa. Isn't that right?" He's a wise man, but I saw he was puzzled. Why was I talking about desertion? I didn't explain.

I have a tiny kitchen where I make the same cheese blintzes Babushka used to make for me. Here I am, on the second floor, the top floor, of a red-roofed, white stucco house in Kibbutz

Broshim, where the windows face endless green fields and beyond them low hills that catch the sun when it sets.

It's a four-family house connected in a neat row to other white stucco houses. The sounds from each apartment are very clear. I can hear the laughter and the arguing. Everything. A kibbutz is like a family. Arguments, rumors, gossip, grandmothers, uncles, sisters, and new family members like me and Lidia. All of us share our food, our work, and the money we earn. And like a family that has a spare room, we invite someone to come live with us for a while. Like Thomas, the volunteer.

Everyone eventually admits to someone what their "real reason" is. Everyone except me. Even Lidia doesn't know about Sergei. I just can't talk about it. Not that I don't think about it. I think about his last minutes; was he scared?

One day Lidia and I were laughing about something that had happened the night before, and suddenly I started crying. That was the moment when I could have said, "Someone promised to love me forever and then he killed himself." But I didn't. How would that sound? Like I was so full of myself, I didn't notice someone else's unhappiness? Sometimes I am afraid it is something about me that has made the men in my life—Sergei, my father—betray me.

The one-story house with the weeping willow shading the front door, across the wide, sweeping lawn from the kibbutz community center, is where Dan's family lives. Dan Oron, born in Israel, tall, black hair shaved close to his scalp, with six more months to serve in the army. When he smiles, you see a chipped front tooth that he got from hitting a diving board. Dan, my soul mate, my love, the reason I can laugh, *the* person I want to spend the rest of my life with. But I am so afraid to give my whole heart.

I want to tell him about Sergei, but I'm terrified he'll think I was to blame. I *will* tell him. I know I have to.

By the time Thomas finishes his volunteer period, we will all know why he came here. To get away from his parents? A huge argument with his girlfriend? Or no girlfriend? High school is a bore? An "interest in Israel"? Or maybe, for Thomas, a struggle with his conscience and his German history? Yes, we will all know why Thomas Wanninger is really here.

When I came to the kibbutz, Baruch was the person I could talk to. He's amazing—he's even older than Babushka, but he listened to me without ever interrupting. He never said I was foolish, or I was young. He was like the grandfather I never knew. I didn't know anything then about Baruch and I still don't. Except of course for the number on his arm. I feel his *oneness* in a place where everyone else is part of *many*. I don't mean lonely, I mean alone. Maybe that's why he's a good listener. And he loves the earth the way I do, the smell of soil, the beauty of seeds growing into fruit and flowers. Dear Baruch, he's taught me everything he learned with his own two hands. "My Odessa princess," he kept saying the first year, "is building a palace in Israel."

Baruch is my grandfather. And Dan, Dan is my heartbeat. When he finishes his army service, he wants to study archaeology. He wants us to go to university together. "I'll have the spade and you'll have the shovel," I said, and we kissed, making it our promise to each other. But I can't forget that this is the second time in my life I've made a promise to someone. Maybe I can't keep it. Maybe I'll let Dan down. Maybe Dan will stop loving me.

I look at my watch. Time to grab breakfast. Meet Lidia for a cup of coffee. Remind Baruch I won't be in the packing house to help with the orders of flowers to be shipped to Holland. I've got to leave for the airport by nine.

6:45 AM Lidia Adler Darkroom, Kibbutz Broshim community center

The photograph was perfect. There was nothing to crop. I had posed Vera sitting on a high stool in the packing shed, her feet balanced on the bottom rung, holding a bouquet of the lilacs she had planted, her Odessa lilacs. The morning sun highlighted her blond hair and lit her cheeks. The photograph is her birthday gift to Dan. I gave it to her yesterday.

No time to think about lilacs. I still have all those kibbutz kindergarten pictures to develop.

Thomas Wanninger El Al flight 01: SXF–TLV (Berlin–Tel Aviv) 6:45 AM

This is the dream I've had for the last few months: I'm in a train. There are no windows. There are other people squeezed against me, pushing me, pressing me. A baby is crying. I can smell their breath, the sweat from their hair, the wet wool of their coats. The brakes screech loudly and the train jerks to a halt. I am thrown backward and forward and backward. All the people disappear from the train, I don't know how, because the door is not rolled open. A woman pats my shoulder and says I'm safe. Where is my mother? I ask. Where is Mutti? I don't know, the woman answers, but come with me. That's when I wake up.

The baby in the third row is crying. The flight attendant brings the mother a blanket. It takes me a few minutes to really wake up. I *am* on a plane and I *am* on my way to Israel. That's what's real.

Ilse Wanninger Aachener Strasse 366, Berlin 6:30 AM (BERLIN TIME)

Dear Tommi,

I hope you have settled in by the time you get this. I want you to know that I do understand why you are doing this, for yourself and maybe also for your father.

In my heart I think Opa Hans caused your father's cancer. Those cancer cells were fed by the fear and shame your father felt. I know this is a terrible thing to say, but maybe the cancer was your father's atonement.

Uncle Friedrich made his once-a-year phone call

yesterday. I remember each time you said that, Papa would laugh.

He called to say the family had decided, after all, to give us the cottage in the country. This is because we "only" have an apartment in Berlin and no place to vacation. Maybe now he won't look down on us anymore.

I told him you went to the kibbutz. His only answer was that you are a "Jew lover" like your father. That obviously you are trying to make up for German sins.

"Tommi doesn't know anything about German sins. He's proud of this country," I told him.

Of course he doesn't believe me. The family is putting up a memorial for Opa Hans in the village cemetery of Lunzrieger, where he was born.

I also want to finally know the truth. Even if you and I are scared of it, we must know what happened. Tommi, go ahead with your plan—use the information and the photographs we copied. Do not concern yourself with Papa's family.

Another thing to tell you: Christina left a message. She feels bad about what she said to you. I think you should write to her.

Love, Mutti

7:30 AM **Baruch Ben Tov** Kibbutz Broshim, Judean Hills

For Thomas Wanninger, notes and advice:

You will be starting your volunteer service during one of the most pleasant times of the year. The drier weather of April is very good for gardening. Spading, mixing compost into the soil, raking flowers and vegetable beds, all will be done this month. This is also the perfect time for planting.

Before the first mowing of the kibbutz lawns, all stones, shrub and tree branches, and lumps of heavy soil must be removed. Remove all seeds. Use a rake or lawn broom. Do not hesitate to ask me any questions about equipment or irrigation.

There are many rosebushes planted all over the kibbutz grounds. They will have to be protected from fungus diseases (like mildew and black spot) and certain insects (beetles, caterpillars, aphids). This protection is done by dusting the rosebushes with sulfur powder or a weekly aerosol spray of Malathion. This is a continuing job that you will do on your own or with the help of a kibbutz member.

When you walk around the outskirts of the kibbutz, you will come to a grove of pine trees and three stone benches. This is the Broshim memorial grove. Over the years kibbutz members have planted trees in memory of people who have passed away—a parent, a child, a soldier, or a person who was dear to a kibbutz member. I like this grove area to be kept spotless.

If you hike to the surrounding neighborhoods of Jerusalem, you will see clusters of strange-looking, big wild plants, thick with thorns and with pretty red, pink, blue, or purple flowers. These are thistles. They will make a nice and long-lasting decoration for your room. But watch out for the thorns when you pick them.

You will be helping with many different gardening tasks. Do not hesitate to ask me questions or for help. I hope you will enjoy your stay with us.

Baruch Ben Tov, Head Gardener

I walk from the plant nursery to Thomas's room, number 5, second floor, the guest hostel, and leave my short list of instructions on the table near the bed. I lift the bedside lamp and put a corner of the sheet of paper underneath so it won't accidentally slip to the floor. On the way out I turn and look at the room. The breeze is blowing the curtains, and the sun is gold on the floor and wall. Who wouldn't like it here? I close the door behind me.

7:57 AM Thomas Wanninger El Al flight 01: SXF–TLV (Berlin–Tel Aviv)

My father, Otto Wanninger, was a veterinarian. His clinic was one kilometer from where the Berlin Wall was. When he was alive, we had a tabby cat, Gretel, and a dog, Hänsel, who was a mixture of a schnauzer and a terrier. Gretel got run over, and we buried her in a far corner of a public park. I remember my father lying in his hospital bed saying Hänsel would live longer than he would. Hänsel died six months after my father.

Home. Berlin. It's raining—the sky is steel gray. If my mother went back home before going to work, I know what she's doing. I know because my mother has a routine. Without her routine, she'd be a nervous wreck. Maybe all these automatic things she does save her from thinking about my father, from remembering my little brother, who died when he was two and I was six. My mother has a lot of courage to let me go, because without me at home, all she has is her routine.

She always hangs her raincoat and scarf on one of the wooden pegs nailed in a row on the hall wall. She peers out the window and sees the bird feeder shaking in the wind. She may open the window just to be sure there are no sparrows. She waters the philodendron plant on the sill. She opens the kitchen closet and takes out a teacup and saucer and a cake plate. She'll have her tea and a slice of buttered brown bread and yellow cheese. Today she'll start waiting to hear what I have found out about Opa Hans.

I have to stop. There's a patrol on the road below the grove. I crouch behind the thick trunk of an olive tree. The soldiers' eyes peer around, searching, looking up and down the roadside ditch. They hold their M-16s, but they don't leave the road. I'm so afraid I want to piss. I don't dare stand up. They move past the curve in the road. They're gone.

I take the backpack off and stand up. I do it against the trunk of the tree. I fix my pants, hoist my backpack, and move quickly through the grove. I don't have to cross the road. I know a better way.

I'm a ghost. Now you see me, now you don't. Hard to think I scare anyone. I'm the dishwasher in the diner kitchen, the floor sweeper, the table wiper, the toilet bowl cleaner. I'm sixteen years old, and I live in a small village of Palestinian Arabs.

It's not living in Zebedeid that makes me an illegal worker, it's my age. If I were over forty, with gray hair and a clean record, I would have a work permit and a magnetic card. I would swipe the card through the machine at the border, the machine would click, and I would be legal. You would see me, not see through me.

Invisible, and I can earn only what my boss takes out of his back pocket. The cash he counts out is what I give my mother so we can all live: food for my two brothers and two sisters, my little brother's kidney pills, flour, oil for cooking, money for clothes. I don't need anything. My boss gives me old pants, someone's T-shirt, and whatever food is left over in the kitchen at the end of the day.

All over the world sixteen is paradise, opportunity, girls, cars, everything. I watch television in Omar's house and see sixteen.

Sixteen is the beach, your own room, a cell phone, surfing on waves that never end, different clothes for every day of the week, a refrigerator full of ice cream and chocolates, a mother who waits for you in a kitchen with a washing machine and a dishwasher, and a father who comes home from work. That is sixteen.

Here sixteen is the magic age of death. No children, no responsibilities, no wife. A sixteen-year-old is a walking grave. Why give a job to someone about to die? Kids who explode themselves and kill Israelis have no future, so don't give them a future.

My boss is different. "I need you, you need me, right, Sameh?"

But the Israeli who hands out the magnetic cards says I am a sixteen-year-old terrorist and I will kill myself for a Palestinian homeland. I know your kind, he says, and he doesn't bother to ask me my name.

7:57 AM   Dan Oron An army base somewhere in Israel

Everyone in the unit will miss Roy. Hard to believe he's out. We swore we'd stay in touch. "Six more months, Dan, and you're out too." What a great guy—has a girlfriend, talks about her all the time when they're not together, the way I talk about Vera. Roy plays the guitar, is going trekking in Peru with his girlfriend.

Last night all of us in the platoon lit candles and sat around till late joking and talking about the army. What we're defending and why, whether we'll still be doing this when we are old men. A lot of us have written last letters to our families, to be given to them in case something happens to us. This isn't something we tell our parents, or girlfriends, or anyone. Like we try not to tell them exactly where we are and what we do on patrol. They'd all go crazy. And they wouldn't laugh if we told them our jokes—that kind of humor is just for us, for guys who are scared or dead tired or both.

My mother doesn't think there's anything funny about the

army. She never turns off her radio—she's afraid she'll miss some kind of breaking news bulletin.

So at midnight we sat around singing. Not patriotic stuff, just the songs we sang when we were in school. We felt good. I crawled into bed exhausted and kind of sad that my best buddy would be gone in the morning. I'd be on my own and he'd be starting real life.

We've had a week of intensive patrolling, looking for stashes of arms in the villages around here. Today everyone's headed home; we all got leave. Of course, if something happens, we'll be back.

I'll call Vera when I get on the bus. I know she's on the way to the airport today to pick up a volunteer. Maybe I won't call her, just surprise her when she gets home. I'll wait for her in her room.

Vera Brodsky Cafeteria, Kibbutz Broshim   7:57 AM

I'm waiting for Lidia. A whole group of us have planned a surprise party for Dan's birthday when he gets leave this week. He might bring an army buddy for Lidia. I want her to be as happy as I am.

I can't believe how my life has changed. I put sugar in my coffee and remember my last day in Odessa. . . .

It was ten in the morning. No one else was home. Mama had gone to work for a few hours, Babushka had gone to the Old People's Club, and Irena was in school. The taxi was ordered for five in the afternoon. I sat on my narrow iron bed looking at my old schoolbooks on the shelf. I'd tell Irena they were hers now, whatever she needed.

What should I take to read on the plane? Maybe nothing—I was too nervous to concentrate. I'd buy a magazine at the airport. I stretched out on my bed and stared at the ceiling.

The bedroom Irena and I shared was at the back of our apartment, and we never could escape the gurgling and bubbling of the building's water pipes, which were behind the wall of the closet. I lived in constant fear that they would burst and ruin my clothes, and Irena was terrified that a flood coming through the wall would destroy all her stuffed animals. I covered the old radiator in the room with a towel and used the heat to dry the things I washed by hand. A long, narrow window looked out on the courtyard three floors below. Sometimes I'd lean out and think I could hear the tooting of the tugboats and the horns of freighters anchoring in the port. Beyond the Black Sea was another life.

Outside our room Mama had curtained off part of the long hall for Babushka's bed and the teacart that was her night table. For four years, since my father left, there'd never been enough money to change things in the apartment.

The doorbell rang. I jumped up from the bed. Even our nosy neighbor would be a welcome distraction from the jumble of memories: Sergei, my parents fighting, my father leaving us, Babushka sad and silent most of the time. Four terrible years. I opened the door.

"I didn't know if I should come, Vera. . . ."

In the dim hallway light I saw it was Sergei's mother. She was right, she shouldn't have come. She was the last person I wanted to see. I hated her, and I'm sure it showed on my face. All she and Sergei's father had done was run Sergei down, criticize him for not doing better, tell him he didn't need a girlfriend, he shouldn't commit himself, the future didn't include me or going to Israel. "No, no, no" was all he ever heard out of their mouths. For as long as I could remember, way before we fell in love, I knew he was miserable at home. It was all he talked about. Later, I was the only thing that made him happy.

"I leave in the afternoon. I still have things to do." I choked the words out.

"I understand. I won't bother you. . . ."

She waited. What did she want me to say? That I was to blame for what had happened?

"The taxi is coming at five."

She nodded. "Yes, of course. To the airport. I found this in the bottom drawer of Sergei's dresser." She moved away from the staircase, toward the open door where I stood, and handed me a square white box. "I'm sure he meant it for you. You know you were everything to him. He relied on you."

I took it. "Thank you," I mumbled. I didn't invite her in and I didn't open the box in front of her. We looked at each other without saying a word. I relied on *him,* I wanted to shout at her.

She turned around. She kept her face down. I couldn't see the expression on it. "Take care of yourself, Vera."

I said nothing. I stepped back and closed the door. How she must have hated coming here. Maybe it made her feel better to see me cry. I knew she would have been happy if I had died instead of Sergei. She blamed me for what he did, and she'd never forget it even if I traveled to the ends of the earth. Even if I said, "Don't you understand, by doing what he did, he deserted me," she wouldn't understand. She's his mother. Why should she understand *me?*

I told no one about Sergei's mother coming to see me. I put the white box at the bottom of the backpack with my money and passport.

A taxi horn honked. I gave Babushka one more hug, kissed Irena and then my mother. The taxi horn honked again. I opened the window. "I'm coming," I yelled down. I saw my father waiting near the taxi. Then I saw his car parked behind it. He huddled in a dark gray woolen coat, his fur hat pulled low and his gloved hands cupped together. Had Mama told him when I was leaving? He didn't look up at our window. He was ashamed to let us see his face. What a coward.

Irena hoisted the backpack onto my shoulders, and she and

Mama walked down the stairs with me. The square suitcase I carried bumped against the side of my leg. It hurt.

At the entrance my mother looked quickly at my father standing near the taxi. "No need for me to go out to the street, Verushka." She held me close for a long time.

"Kiss Babushka again for me."

"Be careful, Verushka, be careful." She did not look out at the street. She kissed me on both cheeks and went inside.

My father came toward me and tried to take my suitcase.

I didn't let go of it. "What are you doing here?"

"Verushka, do you really think I could let you go away without coming to say goodbye?"

"Why didn't you bring *her*? Doesn't she want to see one of your daughters leaving Odessa?"

"Vera, Vera, when you're older, you'll understand. It wasn't just me. Both your mother and I were—"

"If I get to be a hundred, Papa, I'll never blame Mama. You ruined our family."

The taxi driver rolled down the window and pointed to his watch. "No time," he said.

"I know, I know," I answered.

"Let me take you to the airport, Verushka," said my father. "Please."

"How can you even think I want to be with you? You know what I feel. My whole life you've lied to me—about being a Jew, about being a Brodsky. And then what you did to Mama, to Irena and me. How can I get in a car with you? Do you think a hug and a kiss five minutes before I go can make up for all these years?"

He put his hand on my shoulder. "I love you, Verushka. Forgive me for a few minutes, a half hour, whatever time it takes for me to drive you to the airport. Please."

I looked down at the ground and then up at the window. I saw Mama and Irena. Was Mama shaking her head "no" or was she nodding "yes"?

"Please," he said again. I didn't look at him, but I handed him my suitcase. He gave the driver a few bills and said, "It's okay, I'll drive my daughter." Then he opened the trunk of his car and put my suitcase in. I slid into the front passenger seat. He tipped his thick hat, smiled, and asked, "Where to, Miss?"

I didn't smile back. "Central Airport," I said, as if he were a stranger. The car pulled away from the curb. As we became part of the traffic, I looked up again, for the last time, at our window. Mama and Irena were staring down at the street. I started to cry. I took my woolen glove off and wiped away the tears.

"I know leaving Odessa is hard for you, Verushka."

"You don't know anything," I said.

He patted my hand. I moved it away. Luckily he didn't say any more. I was grateful for the silence. Did he honestly know how hard this was? The two men I most adored in my life had cut my heart open. I wanted to tell him I was scared, I would never heal, I would never get over everything that had happened. I was a cripple and I had to learn to walk again. These were my first steps, and they hurt.

I rolled down the window and leaned out and looked back. The apartment building got smaller and more distant as the car sped up the avenue. There was the place where the old ladies from the countryside sold fresh vegetables, where they stacked their crates of cucumbers and lettuce and spread out bunches of grapes. Papa turned the corner.

I drank in the sight of the streets: Pushkinskaya, with the music conservatory; my favorite department store on Rishelevska; Ekaterinskaya, where Galina lives, where Sergei's family lives; and at its end, the Pryvoz market. I looked at all the places like a person who may go blind any minute. Remember this, remember that. I would miss it, but deep down I knew I had to leave. Really, I was glad to be leaving. Odessa was already covered in evening shadows, the winter darkness would not disappear until the next morning. Here and there someone walked on the avenue under the row of plane trees or hurried across the boulevard. The wind bent everyone in two. Look, Vera, look. You may never come back.

The buildings we sped by were painted blue or deep gold, with balconies that sprouted out from every one of the three or four stories. The entrances had heavy wooden doors, and sculptured flower garlands cut out of stone decorated the long windows. This was not faraway Moscow, it was my beautiful Odessa, but now, for me, it was dead.

Too much pain, too many people who disappointed me, like Sergei and Papa. Too many hours of crying, too much loneliness. *"Zhidovka"*—"the Jew girl"—I heard my classmates whisper when they found out I had changed my name. Everyone is equal, everyone is the same, my teachers would parrot. But I knew otherwise. I knew about the years when Jews were sentenced to death for trying to emigrate to Israel, jailed even for praying in a synagogue.

I was leaving for Israel, even if it was dangerous to live there, because there I could be proud of what I was. And it was Alex Ushakov, who used to be Brodsky, driving me to the airport.

I look at my watch. It's getting late, I think. Then I see Lidia come into the cafeteria.

8:10 AM Thomas Wanninger El Al flight 01: SXF–TLV (Berlin–Tel Aviv)

One day after my father died, I sat at the desk in the study staring at his photograph. Now it was Mutti and me. I would help her with the accounts, with closing my father's veterinary clinic, maybe we'd move to a smaller apartment. I started to open the desk drawers. I don't know why I did this; I had never done it before. I can't explain what I was looking for, but I had a feeling there would be something there, something he and Mutti hadn't wanted me to see. Don't parents hide things from children because they're children?

In the middle drawer I found the photographs. There were three fuzzy black-and-white pictures of lines of people and a row of soldiers in uniforms. Then there was the other photograph, quite clear, of Opa Hans in his army uniform.

I got it. Someone was saying: look for this man, he's in *all* the pictures. He's part of what's going on. Look hard, he's there. I looked but didn't see him.

I put the pictures back in the envelope that had no return address and closed the drawer. I didn't say anything to Mutti. I didn't say anything to anyone. Later that week I opened the drawer once again. I had to make sure I hadn't been imagining the photographs. And again I wondered, was my grandfather there?

I started reading about Israel and the Jews. Almost every afternoon I'd go to the school library. There were at least five shelves with books on Jewish history, Jewish legends and stories, the reasons for anti-Semitism, the rise of Hitler, the history of the Second World War. The war books had photographs of German soldiers, of officers, doing terrible things. Men wearing the same uniform as Opa kicking children and old men, prodding women like Mutti to undress in the street. In many of the pictures the uniformed men were smiling.

My life changed. I knew I couldn't tell anyone about the photographs, not Rudi, not Christina. I knew about something, something bad, and it buzzed around in my head all the time. I'd be talking to someone, but a section of my brain had this thing, this piece of information, and it choked everything else. One part of me standing in the cafeteria talking was okay, the other part was like a robot. How could Opa Hans have done that? How could any human being do it? Rewind, play, rewind, play, his photograph kept running through my head. In my mind the photograph of him had a title—Nazi war criminal. Sixty years ago, part of German history, part of my family, my father's father. Whenever I could, I'd open the drawer and take out the envelope. I searched for his face in the three grainy black-and-white photographs but couldn't find anyone who looked like him.

These things that had happened were now part of me, part of my life, in my bones, inherited. I had inherited evil. Could a person have evil genes? Adults say youth is innocent. What a joke.

I kept on doing everything I always did: went to soccer practice, went out with everyone for pizza, hung around with Christina. I told myself the only way to keep from going crazy was to go on acting normal. But Christina noticed. She was sure I was keeping something from her. She got angry I wasn't telling her what was going on. "I want to help you, Tommi, but you won't talk to me. You're different now. I know it's about your father and I want to help. If you love me, if we love each other, you'll tell me everything. People who love each other don't have secrets. I tell *you* everything."

The horror of what I imagined, of what my grandfather, my own grandfather, Opa Hans, might have done to other human beings, paralyzed me. I thought about it all the time. My friends and teachers were sure my moods were because of my father's death.

Mutti was asked to come to school. The day before, on a Sunday afternoon, I told her I knew what was in the middle drawer of the desk. She was surprised, and then she said, "I'm glad—it's about time you knew everything."

Finally I had someone to share my questions with. She said she was sorry Papa had never told me about the photographs, and how they had arrived in the mail with no name or return address, only a Hamburg postmark. I was too young, Papa said, to know about this. Everyone was in the army, Mutti said, but some soldiers fought on the front lines and some soldiers did "other things." That's what worried Papa. Ate at him.

She went to the meeting with my counselor and told him I needed a change from the school routine. She was willing to let me travel—maybe there was a volunteer program in Israel. The counselor told us about SEEK. She never mentioned the real reason to the counselor. Anyway, all the school cared about was that I had her permission and some kind of educational goal.

And all I cared about was that Kibbutz Broshim was near Jerusalem. "There's a place in Jerusalem, Mutti, I read about it in one of the books, that has testimonies of Jewish victims. That is the only place that might have some record of him. Once and for all we will know the truth about Opa Hans."

But even though my mother found out about the SEEK program, when it came to the moment for her to give her permission for me to go, she backed down. "You're all I have, Tommi. If I lose you . . . We can call this institute, we can fax them, why do you have to go?"

"Because it's more than just finding out what my grandfather did—it's making up for it, being there. It's an apology, me asking for forgiveness."

"You can't walk around a country telling people you're sorry. That's just ridiculous!"

"That's not what I'm going to do. By being there, by trying to understand the Jews, *that* will be like saying I'm sorry. Don't you understand?"

"But you weren't even born then."

"My name is Wanninger, isn't it?"

We looked at the photographs again and again, trying to make sense of them. But without going to this place in Jerusalem, this Yad Vashem, we would have no explanation.

"The principal approves of this SEEK program, you said so yourself, Mutti."

"Yes, he does."

"That's all I need, an excuse, a reason to go there. Please."

She began to give in. She backed up my request for school leave, even though I'd be missing end-of-term exams.

There are two paperbacks in my backpack. One is a history of the Jews and the other is a guidebook to Israel. I'm too charged up and jittery to read them now. Later, maybe. I can't believe I'm on the plane, on my way. If I could jump out of the plane and push it, make it go faster, I would. Nothing is important to me anymore, only discovering the truth. What will I do after that? I don't know.

The flight attendant announces a movie. I pull down the window shade, put on the earphones, and press my seat into the "recline" position. Other passengers are switching off their overhead lights. A movie will make this flight seem shorter. The screen is lowered from the ceiling. A train speeds across the screen. The movie title flashes over the railroad cars. Three men are running down the corridor of this movie train with guns in their hands. I think I've heard about this movie—it's a thriller or something. It looks pretty dumb.

I press the backpack lock, throw back the flap, and put my hand in to check if the manila envelope is still there. Of course it is. I look inside and see the rectangular shape of the cardboard I cut to keep the photographs from bending. If it suddenly disappeared from my backpack, there would be no reason for me to be on this plane.

From the minute I opened the drawer, there wasn't a day when I didn't think about Opa Hans, his photograph, and imagine what he did. I even found an article, in a book about photography, about army photographers during the Second World War.

The army photographer assigned to the battalion posed, photographed, and developed hundreds of soldiers' pictures: photographs of soldiers receiving medals, being decorated for bravery or efficiency, ceremonies of promotion, all the standard commemoration that makes the Fatherland and the soldier's family proud.

The photographer had his standards. There must be clarity of detail: the rank on the shoulder, the crisp outline of the cap or hat or helmet, the knotted tie smartly concealing the top shirt button. If this soldier was killed in battle, there must be something of pride left to display on the mantelpiece of the bereaved family. This was the purpose of photography, to show the truth without words. There was no higher truth—photography was not mechanical transcription, it was art.

It was scary how exactly that article described my grandfather's photograph, the one he had sent home. Another print of it had arrived in an envelope with the three other photographs. Who else knew Opa?

I take the earphones off. The movie continues: A holdup, people jump off the train, there's a fire in one of the cars. There are frightened people crouching under the seats, banging on the closed railroad car windows, it's a robbery or a kidnapping. The men are wearing ski masks and waving machine guns. I close my eyes and I see the movie that's in my head: soldiers, German soldiers and boxcars, not upholstered seats, and more German soldiers. Someone is playing a trick on me, or maybe I'm playing a trick on myself, because I'm seeing Opa Hans in every scene.

The baby in the front section of the plane is crying again. I open my eyes. The lights in the cabin are off—everyone is watching the movie. My dream about the train comes back into my head. I've got to get it out of there. I pull the window shade up and stare at the clear morning sky and think about the last time I saw Christina.

*   *   *

It was Friday night and her parents were out. Her brother was at a basketball game. We'd made up, the argument about my going to Israel dead and buried. As far as Christina knew, I was going to Israel because I needed to get away, to take a break from all the sadness, my mother's crying, all that stuff. We loved each other, and when I got back, I'd be the same old Tommi.

But then she started to tease me. "You won't let them turn you into a Jew, will you, Tommi?"

I could feel her breath against my neck, and her hair brushed against my cheek. I loved her so much, but she wouldn't let go of this stupidity about Jews and Israel. I didn't want to argue again. I didn't want to tell her why I was really going. I couldn't until I got back with the answer I was looking for.

"Tommi, why don't you answer me?" She laughed and kissed me. "Don't tell me you *want* to become Jewish?"

I moved away from her. "You know, Christina, that's dumb."

She got up from the couch. "Sure, like *you* don't say or do dumb things. I'm here for you when you're going through everything and then you take off for Israel. As if being away from me is exactly what you need."

"Can you stop saying all these things? You mean everything to me. You saved me when my father was so sick. If you hadn't been around . . ."

"So why are you going away? I don't understand it, Tommi. And you know what, I don't understand you. It's like you're doing this just to spite me because I don't fall over myself feeling sorry for Jews. So what if I don't? At least I'm honest."

"Why are you making fun of me? What's so ridiculous about going to Israel? Do you think this is so easy for me? Well, it's not. And you're not making it any easier. If this is the way you love me, well, thanks but no thanks. This is who I am, Christina."

We were both standing. We looked at each other and for what seemed like forever we didn't say anything. It wasn't like in the movies, where a phone rings or someone walks in. It was just the two of us, staring at each other and I think knowing it was all about to be over.

"I like who I am, Tommi, and I'm not going to change for anyone."

"Me neither," I said. I took my jacket and left.

I thought I'd call Christina the day before the flight, but I didn't. Rudi told me she just shrugged her shoulders when he asked her what had happened between us.

Baruch Ben Tov Garden equipment shed, Kibbutz Broshim   *8:10 AM*

I see the bee outside the equipment-shed window. It quivers over a dark purple iris, then dives in. It's almost lost in the flower. I crane my neck—ah, there it is. The sun is flooding the shed, lighting the hoes, the rakes, the spades, the scythes, the baskets. And there is the smell of clods of earth and the smell of stems and petals. Why does this comfort me, make that tattooed number on my arm burn less? So many years, and still . . . Only the hedges and grasses, the flowers, the bushes, the sweet-smelling lawn of this place can comfort me. They grow, they sprout, they blossom, and they conceal everything that is ugly. These growing things I learned to plant with my own two hands because they don't carry the smell of death.

I grew up in a three-story brick house. Six families lived in that house. There was a square where the street curved. It had two linden trees. My memories are colored gray and red and brown and black, not green, the green I see every morning when I wake, the hills that stretch to the horizon.

If I could, I would plant a flower for every child so willfully murdered, for Anny, for Roza, for Manya, for Lelka, for Surcis, for Rivka, for Alexander, for Edward, for George, for Marek, for Lea, for Sergio, for Bette, for Jacqueline, for Eleanora, for Eva, for Gabriel, for Edward, for Benjamin, the children I knew, the children I didn't know. A meadow of one million flowers, for all of them, for all of them. That is why I am a gardener.

Ilse Wanninger Aachener Strasse 336, Berlin

The one thing Otto found hard to talk about with me was his father and his disappearance. From the moment we met, we opened our hearts to each other, but anything about his father was a closed door. He found it hard to say "My father died in the war." I remember our first date: He said his father had disappeared, had been reported missing. I didn't understand then what he was afraid to tell me. As if he had a premonition that his father was something other than a regular German soldier. Like everyone else.

All I knew about my father-in-law was that he had been very proud and patriotic. He wasn't young enough to be in the infantry or in a tank division, so he enlisted to serve in a special unit. His army service was to keep the local populations under control, to show the people of the countries the Germans occupied who was winning the war. The army unit was known as the Reserve Police, and he had served as a policeman in Poland. Though he knew nothing about firearms—he had been a bookkeeper all his life—he was prepared to do anything for the Fatherland. No one, though, knew exactly what he had done as a Reserve Policeman. And the soldier Hans Wanninger had disappeared into thin air.

I tried to talk to Otto's mother about it. I would look at the army photograph of Otto's father and comment on how Otto resembled him. She always smiled and agreed with me. "Otto's brothers look like my side of the family, but Otto looks like his father," she said. Many times I asked her what she thought had happened to her husband, how a soldier could be missing for so many years, did she still have hope his body would be found?

She was a wonderful woman, generous and kind to me, but talking about her husband, the war, or what had happened to him was *verboten*—forbidden. She always had the same answer for me: *"Ich werde nicht fragen, warum und weshalb"*: I will not ask why and what for. To question what had happened to her husband would blacken the memory of all those German soldiers who had served the Fatherland. Her refusal, like the slamming of a door, would end our conversation.

When he was a little boy, Tommi would ask, "Where is Opa?"

She would pat his head and say, *"Dies werde ich mit ins Grab nehmen"*: I will take this with me to my grave.

And he, not understanding, would say, "Oh, Oma, then I'll wait till the day *before* you die. You'll tell me then, won't you?"

"Of course, of course," she said, but I knew whatever it was she didn't want to talk about would still remain her secret.

Her death seemed to release Otto from some kind of bond or promise he had made. We began making inquiries into what had happened to Reserve Officer Hans Wanninger, missing in action somewhere in Poland, 1942. Otto's brothers refused to help. Even when Otto shouted at them to tell him what they knew, they would say only that their father had died a hero's death somewhere on the eastern front. They would have no part in trying to dishonor his name with postwar political nonsense.

We sent letters to the *Deutsches Rotes Kreuz,* but the Red Cross had no record of him, and even to *Der Volksbund Deutscher Kriegsgräberfürsorge,* an association that cares for soldiers' graves. We placed a classified ad in the newspapers. No response. All we had was the one photograph he had sent to his wife and sons. A veterans' organization had a single listing, just his name: *Ordnungspolizei / Battalion 304 / Hans Wanninger.* There was nothing more until the photographs arrived, how and why we didn't know.

Not many people on the bus. I'm sitting in the front, near the door, as I always do. Someone at the kibbutz once told me it's the safest place to sit in a bus. The trip to the airport takes about an hour and a half.

The wide windows of the bus remind me of the airport bus in Odessa that took the passengers from the terminal to the plane bound for Tel Aviv. I remember . . . that day I left . . . talking to Babushka.

"I wouldn't tell this to anyone before, but I'm scared. I didn't mean to do this, to leave, on my own. It always was going to be Sergei and me, going off together. Who am I, now that he's gone?"

"You're strong and independent."

"I'm not, Babushka, I'm not. Sergei's dead. Why? He had all sorts of thoughts, about his life, maybe about us, and he never told me. How can you love and not share? Even committing suicide he thought only about himself, his pain. Not about me. He abandoned me. The same way Papa abandoned us."

"Your questions will be answered by the passing of time. Time solves everything."

"It doesn't. Nothing gets solved by time. Things only hurt more. What you're saying is the answer of old people."

"Yes." She sighed. "Because we have experience."

"But *now* I hear his voice, *now* I feel his hand in my hand, holding me. He is with me all the time, but he doesn't answer my question: Why did you leave me?

"I loved him so much. We're going to Israel together, he said. I miss him, Babushka, so badly. But I can't stay here. And then Papa and that young woman . . . Foolish Mama, who still loves him, and sweet Irena, who doesn't know what a liar he is. He changed even his own name, his heritage. Oh, Babushka, why don't people you love tell you the truth?"

"Your papa will or won't come to his senses. And Sergei—well, Sergei wanted everything to be perfect in a perfect world. What he did had nothing to do with you. Don't think that, even for a minute. You, my sweet granddaughter, are like a seed in the wind. You will grow and blossom, bloom in whatever field you are blown to. At the kibbutz people will love you and see how wonderful you are. No one abandoned you and no one will *ever* abandon you. Give me a hug and go finish your packing."

Central Airport, Odessa, was old, not like the airports you see in American movies. In Los Angeles or New York everything is steel, shiny, well-dressed people rushing here and there, all so busy and important. Of course, they live in the center of the world. Here an old lady with a twig broom was sweeping the floor in large repetitious circles.

Five passengers were collecting their luggage from a cart. I could see by the stickers that they had arrived from Tel Aviv. I wanted to ask them what Israel was like, was Tel Aviv large, would someone understand my Russian, my English? Were people friendly?

Their suitcases were battered brown imitation leather with broken corners and twine wound around them. Probably the locks did not close well. I could see the cardboard frame underneath the fake leather. They had brought back bags of clothing, and large dolls, and cellophane-covered boxes of toys. How would they get all of this home? Where did they live, what neighborhood of Odessa would they be taking these packages and bundles to?

The cleaning lady swept around them, and I saw her looking with envy at the clothing and toys. Was she saying to herself, "Those rich Jews"?

My suitcase and backpack were examined.

"What is this?" the security officer asked, pointing to the bottom of the backpack.

I took out the square white box Sergei's mother had given me. "It's a present."

"Open it."

I wanted to explain that I was waiting to open it when I got to Israel. But I did as I was told. He took out a silver heart on a chain and dangled it from his hand. It swung from side to side. I wasn't going to cry in front of this man. I bit my lips.

"See, a present. I told you."

His finger moved around the edge of the heart looking for the catch. "Drugs, you kids are always hiding drugs."

He snapped the locket open. A piece of paper fell out on the counter. I grabbed it and smoothed the small square. It was Sergei's handwriting. *Lyube vsem syertsem. Nye boysya zavtrashnego dnya. Prosti menya. Sergei.* Love with all your heart. Don't be afraid of tomorrow. Forgive me. Sergei.

The officer looked embarrassed. He placed the locket in the palm of my hand. Both my hands were shaking as I pushed open the clasp on the chain necklace. I put it on. I folded the paper and pressed it into the open locket and then snapped it shut. It would always be with me.

My bags were weighed and tags attached. I went to the passport booth.

"Vera Brodsky?" the immigration official asked. His nose was stuck into the pages of my passport; his glasses had slid down almost to his chin. He did not see me nod. I did not say anything, I did not move. He turned a page and squinted at my picture in the passport. There was nothing wrong with his eyes. He was an official, and officials enjoy making you understand how important they are. I waited. He was winning this little war of nerves; he turned the pages of my passport from front to back, from back to front. I prepared to answer questions about my father's name. I began to see myself in the taxi on the way back home, my departure denied.

Again he asked, "Vera Brodsky?"

Don't annoy him, I said to myself. "Yes," I answered with great politeness and respect.

"Long hair in the photo," he said, and looked intently at my short hair.

"But the same color, blond," I pointed out.

Silence. He continued to look at me and at the passport picture.

I explained. "I cut it one month ago, after the passport was issued. If you want, I'll grow a braid again." A minute after I made the joke, I wanted to kick myself.

He didn't laugh. He shrugged, stamped the passport, and slid it back to me. I passed through the swinging door and boarded the airport bus.

The bus driver stops for two soldiers. They climb up the bus stairs. They look tired. I think of Dan, on patrol, on a base, somewhere. I hope he's safe. They squeeze sideways down the bus aisle, their duffel bags and rifles bumping against the sides of the seats. They sit in the empty seat behind me. The door closes; the bus continues to Ben Gurion Airport.

Sameh Laham Judean Hills   9:15 AM

My backpack is heavy and I'm moving much more slowly than I usually do. I'm past the olive groves and a small pine forest. Now I'm standing behind a cluster of thistles, looking down at a wide road. The morning traffic is heavy, many cars going in both directions. This is the road that leads to the intersection. Below, a tank and two armored cars drive along the shoulder of the road. In the back of one of the armored cars the soldiers are eating pita. Helmeted soldiers' heads are sticking out of the tank hatch—their rifles are cocked. They would shoot me just for the fun of it, but they don't see me.

I look at my watch. I have to hurry. The Boss is waiting for me.

Thomas Wanninger El Al flight 01: SXF–TLV (Berlin–Tel Aviv)

Another hour until we land. We're flying over the Mediterranean. Every once in a while there are islands below. I take out the guidebook:

> The Israeli work week begins with Sunday, and the only day of rest is Saturday—the Sabbath. Tuesday, the third day of the week, is considered a lucky day. The origin of this belief is the Bible. In the description of the creation, God creates the earth and the oceans and sees that it is good. He then creates plants and trees of every kind. God says again how good it is. Twice God has said that the third day is "good." No other day in the week of creation is mentioned this way. So for centuries Jews have come to believe that the third day, Tuesday, is a lucky day.

Too bad I didn't know this. I could have gotten a flight on Tuesday. Well, maybe I'll find out about Opa on a Tuesday.

Interrogation room, police headquarters, Jerusalem

OMAR JOULANI: Why am I here again?

POLICE OFFICER: Why aren't you in Jabel Fahm? What are you doing here in Jerusalem? Working illegally? Found an Israeli who wants cheap labor? Tell us his name and you'll get out of here now.

OMAR JOULANI: Someone stopped me near the Street of the Prophets. That's all I know.

POLICE OFFICER: That isn't what I asked. Listen to me—I'm not talking some strange language, get it? I'm talking Arabic. You understand me, don't you?

OMAR JOULANI: Yes.

POLICE OFFICER: Good. I want to know why and how you got back into Jerusalem. And all you do is tell me about the Street of Prophets. That's not what I asked.

OMAR JOULANI: This guy stopped me in the street and told me he needed help moving some furniture. He told me he'd give me a few shekels if I helped him.

POLICE OFFICER: Your story is a lie. A man stopped you in the street. Just like that? Stopped you and offered you work? Didn't ask you where you come from, if you have a work card, nothing?

OMAR JOULANI: Not everyone hates Palestinians, you know. What's so strange about an Israeli offering me some work?

POLICE OFFICER: There's nothing strange about it. What's strange is that you're back in Jerusalem when a police car took you to your grandfather's vegetable stall in Jabel Fahm at seven-thirty. Maybe you're back here because you're waiting for your friend Sameh.

OMAR JOULANI: I'm not waiting for anyone. All I want to do is earn some money.

POLICE OFFICER: So you came all the way back to Jerusalem. That's taking a big chance. And who's the person who brought you? You didn't walk. You didn't have enough time.

OMAR JOULANI: An Israeli.

POLICE OFFICER: The same person who needs your help moving?

OMAR JOULANI: No, another man.

POLICE OFFICER: What kind of car?

OMAR JOULANI: Don't remember.

POLICE OFFICER: Passenger car, pickup, truck, what was it? What color?

OMAR JOULANI: Didn't look.

POLICE OFFICER: You're a stupid liar, Omar. You're so stupid, you think I'll believe any story you tell me. No Israeli gave you a lift, and no Israeli needs help moving. You're here looking for Sameh Laham or waiting for him.

OMAR JOULANI: I'm not.

POLICE OFFICER: Ben, fingerprint and photograph him.

OMAR JOULANI: You already have my fingerprints and photograph.

POLICE OFFICER: So now you're a policeman. You know how we work. So, we'll take your picture and fingerprints *again*. Okay with you?

OMAR JOULANI: Do what you want.

POLICE OFFICER: Listen, Omar, and listen carefully. Once you're in our computer, you're marked. You can't ever escape. If you're a bad boy, we'll find you. So be a good boy, help your grandfather sell vegetables and go to school. Then nothing will happen to you.

OMAR JOULANI: Are you sure, Mr. Policeman?

POLICE OFFICER: I'm sure, Omar.

9:30 AM **Dan Oron** An army base somewhere in Israel

I'm in the line waiting to get on the bus. Some of the guys are squatting in the shade of a eucalyptus tree, smoking and talking on their cell phones. The trees remind me of the long road leading to the main gate of Broshim, lined with eucalyptus trees. God, I'm homesick. I really miss Vera.

I'm trying to convince Guy that Vera's friend Lidia Adler is worth meeting, so he'll spend part of his leave at Broshim. "She's great. Not tall, shorter than you, dark hair, comes from Argentina—"

"Danny, you're making me nervous, you're talking too much about this girl. Does she speak Hebrew?"

I switch the cell phone to my other ear, the connection keeps breaking up. "Of course she speaks Hebrew. She's been at the kibbutz three years—she's staying. Believe me, she's a real firecracker. Hot salsa dancer, studies photography, life of the party, come on, you know these Argentinians—they've got batteries that run twenty-four hours a day. Look, she's my girlfriend's best friend. You'll love her."

"I'll try and make it, but I'm not promising. I've got a hundred things to do at home. You said we'd go surfing, remember? Anyway, I have a feeling you're fixing me up just to make your girlfriend happy."

"I keep telling you, Vera is a very picky girl from Odessa. If she's crazy about Lidia, well, then she's something. And, hey, I know her also. The two of you are made for each other. Take my word for it. And we'll go surfing, I swear."

"Who knows when we'll get leave again, Danny." I hear his voice change. He's giving in. "Okay, look, I'll go to the kibbutz, but if this Lidia's a thumbs-down, you'll owe me a really big favor."

"Trust me."

I click the phone shut. Guy drives me crazy. He's the best sharpshooter in the unit, but when it comes to girls, he's as shy as a snail hiding in his shell. Of course the idea of asking him was Vera's, but I conveniently forgot to tell him that. Anyway, I'm sure he'll like Lidia.

Sameh Laham Yoni's Diner, Highway 1   9:35 AM

"*Ahlan v'Sa'alam*, Sameh."

"*Shalom*, Boss."

The Boss likes to show me he is friendly, so he always throws in words of Arabic to let me know he has no hard feelings about me or my kind. I always answer in Hebrew because it shows him I know who is boss. He *is* my boss. A real boss, the Boss of my life because he is Israeli.

"Omar was here in a yellow van, Sameh. He said to tell you he came by."

45

"Yes, I sent him to deliver the message."

"He did. He told me your mother was ill and you were trying to take her to a doctor."

"Yes, that's it, Boss."

"So, you're here. She's better."

"Yes, she's better."

"Have your backpack with you? Your clothes, whatever?"

I show the Boss I have all my things with me.

"Good. It was tough cleaning up, the week you weren't here. Put your things in the broom closet."

My mother was a beautiful woman. In her wedding picture she's tall, eighteen years old, black hair curled and falling on her shoulders, eyes as shiny as crystal pieces. Now she walks slowly from a pain in her legs that never seems to go away. There is nothing shiny about her anymore, not her hair, not her eyes. Nothing. The scarf that covers her hair is pulled across her eyes when she wants no one to see her cry. And my father. In the wedding picture he is tall, with a reddish mustache, wearing a dark jacket and white pants. He does not look comfortable in those clothes. But a farmer is not used to fancy clothes. The picture does not tell about his cancer and my mother's sadness. It is the picture before the bad things happened to us.

"Start with the kitchen floor, Sameh, before the noon rush."

"Yes, Boss."

My boss has *his* wedding picture on the wall of the diner. He also has a large photograph of his oldest son in a soldier's uniform. The boy is a real hero, he likes to tell me. I don't ask how he became a hero. He will end his army service soon. But he will always be a hero. I bet he won't clean toilets afterward. I don't even really look at the picture. I just pretend to.

Below me are small and large dots of land. The Greek islands, the pilot announces. They have the green-brown color of maps in a geography book. I go back to my guidebook:

> Hebrew is the language of the State of Israel. Arabic is spoken by the Arab population. Jews who immigrated to Israel from Muslim countries still speak a variety of Arabic dialects. Many words in Arabic and Hebrew share common roots, for example the words for "peace"—*Sa'alam* and *Shalom*. But other words, such as the Arabic word for "land," *bilad,* are not similar; the Hebrew word for "land" is *eretz.*

My chances of meeting an Arab or needing to know any words in Arabic are zero. I flip to a page I've read a hundred times—I almost know it by heart.

> Yad Vashem is the official State of Israel memorial museum to the victims of Nazi terror. It contains archives with carefully verified names and dates of Jews exterminated in the concentration camps, Jewish partisans killed by the Nazis, towns destroyed by the German army, and records of the non-Jews who did not cooperate with the Nazis. It also contains witness statements identifying Nazi personnel who did and did not perpetrate atrocities. The museum is located in Jerusalem and can be reached by public transport. The museum, exhibits, and archives are open to the public.

This is my true destination. This is where I will discover the truth about my grandfather. I'm sure of it.

For a month after my father died, I couldn't take the bus to school. I had to move, to jog, to run. I had to change my body position from sitting next to my father's bed in the hospital, from hunching over next to my mother in the waiting room.

Taking this trip is getting back to *me,* to my body, to being strong, to not being near sickness and death. Though finding out about Opa Hans is also about death, isn't it?

There's a guy who lives in our apartment building. He's around thirty, works at a bank, I think. Loner. Dark skinned. The name on his mailbox is Rashid Muallem. I don't know where he's from, but I know he isn't a "guest worker." He is too well dressed to be a laborer or work in a shop. He is always under the hood of an old Volkswagen, and half the time I meet him at the bus stop.

"Broke down again?" I said when I saw him last.

"Yeah, the carburetor." He spoke with an accent.

"I'm leaving Berlin for a while, going to Israel," I said. I don't know what made me tell him. Maybe I thought he was from someplace in the Middle East. Maybe I wanted him to smile and say, "Good for you."

"Nice to travel," he said. That was all. Then we got on the bus, and I never did find out if he was Arab or where he was from.

I thought about Rashid Muallem when the guy at the airport gave me my passport back. Maybe I do know someone who speaks Arabic. But I don't really *know* him, do I?

9:35 AM **Vera Brodsky Number 9 bus to Ben Gurion Airport**

The bus slows down and stops for a traffic light on the outskirts of Lod. In half an hour we'll be at the airport. A large metal sign in English and Hebrew tells whoever is interested that Richard the Lionheart rebuilt Lod in the Middle Ages. The town doesn't look very historical, just dusty and boring.

The bus pulls over. The doors open. A Border Patrol soldier armed with an M-16 boards the bus. He nods to the driver.

"Identify your packages," he says to everyone.

Everyone opens their shopping bags, their backpacks, whatever they have. I open my straw shoulder bag. He points to the roll of white cardboard sticking out of my bag. "What's that?"

I unroll it. I read the English lettering: SEEK VOLUNTEER: THOMAS WANNINGER. I can see he does not understand it. I explain. "I'm going to the airport to pick up a foreigner. This is his name. He'll look for me holding up this sign. He doesn't understand Hebrew."

He grins. "Okay. I understand." He says the words in English with a heavy accent and looks around and then laughs. Everyone laughs with him. His attempt at speaking English is funny. He walks down the aisle looking at everyone again and glancing at the overhead luggage shelf. Then he gets off the bus. The bus driver starts the engine, pulls away from the side of the road, and gets back on the highway. I see the soldier standing in the dust of the bus wheels. He is leaning against the sign about Richard the Lionheart.

One of the soldiers sitting behind me says, "What a dump to live in."

I turn around. "You can't always pick where you live," I say.

The other soldier takes off his earphones. "What?"

"She said I shouldn't call this place a hole."

I laugh. "Not exactly," I say.

"Oh, yeah," the soldier says. But he couldn't care less. He doesn't want conversation, just wants to listen to the music.

He holds the earphones in his hand; the Walkman keeps playing. I hear the Beatles singing "She's Leaving Home." I played that the whole month before I left Odessa. I turn around. I see my reflection in the bus window. I can see how much I look like my mother, the same full cheeks (pudgy, I call them), the nose thin, almost a line when I see it in profile like now, nice ears that don't stick out (pretty dumb to admire your own ears), yes, my mother's daughter. Babushka used to call me her second daughter.

What's my father doing now? I wonder. Did he get his position as head of the university physics department? Is he still living with that woman?

I wanted to tell Sergei about her, but for the longest time I was too ashamed. Finally, though, I blurted the whole thing out to him.

After he killed himself, I remembered his answer. It echoed in my head like a scream in a tunnel. "But Verushka, isn't everyone entitled to do with their life what they wish?" Did he mean my father or himself?

"And if they cause pain to others?" I asked.

"We have only one life, we get to decide what to do with it."

"You refuse to understand, Sergei."

"No, Vera, it's you who don't understand. But one day you will."

My father left us, moved out of the apartment. I no longer was the guardian of the secret that would protect my mother from pain. She knew everything—my father had told her. She seemed relieved.

"What a garden of lies we grow," I said to Sergei. "Look at them—picking the flower that smells the best to them." The only thing that made the pain less was knowing I was leaving. Sergei and I together. It was then I decided about my name, my *real* name. My father's *real* name.

I didn't tell Mama. I told Sergei, and I told Babushka.

"If Papa wants nothing to do with us, if he's left us, why should I continue to call myself Ushakov? I am Jewish, the boy I love is Jewish and not ashamed of it, everyone in school assumes I'm Jewish. I may not get the university scholarship because I am Jewish. . . ."

"What are you saying, Verushka?"

"I'm saying, Babushka, I want to change my name to Brodsky, the name my father was born with, the Jewish name his father was exiled for. Just think, every time Papa has to write my name, my full name, it will remind him, *I* will remind him of what he is, of the Jew he was born."

It came out of my mouth as if I'd been thinking about it for years. As if I'd opened the window in the room I shared with Irena and a wind rushed in. It blew away all the small silly things, only the important things remained in place. I would change my name. I would say goodbye to the lies and anger and deceit. In Israel I would be Vera Brodsky.

Mama put a brave face on my whirlwind of decisions. I think she knew there was no way to make me change my mind. She signed all the papers, gave me money from her savings for the ticket, and even resigned herself to seeing me sign "Vera Brodsky" on my new passport.

Irena wanted no part of what she called my craziness. "If Ushakov is good enough for Papa and Mama, it's good enough for me. I don't have to be like you, Vera."

"No, you don't, Irena. I love you as you are. I wouldn't change you for the world." I hugged her and told her I loved her no matter what. Names weren't important, I said.

"So, if it's not important, why *did* you change your name, Verushka?"

I didn't answer my sister. She was too young to understand. But Babushka understood. And Sergei, Sergei always understood.

In the long weeks before I left, all of us tried to stick to the familiar routine of our lives. Mama went to work, brought home exams to mark and other schoolwork, cooked, but at night I heard her crying. Was she still crying for Papa, for her loneliness, or was it for me? I felt bad about being so happy. I was changing my life. I was in love, I had Sergei. She had no one. Then my world crashed.

I will love you always. You are my Vera, here on earth and wherever my spirit will go. I hope my soul will be part of yours in Israel. Everything is dark and my life seems like a hallway of closed doors. I must leave this place, this ugly world. You are counting on me. Don't. I am a weak person, not the strong person you think I am. There is no light—not even your love can light my blackness. I'm sorry. Don't change your plans. Go to Israel as we planned. Be happy always.

Yours forever, Sergei

"Verushka, you are too, too angry," my mother said. "You loved Sergei. Don't change that love to hate."

"Mama, I still don't understand, why did he think it was better to die than to be alive?"

All she could say was "He loved you so much, so much."

And all I could say was "If he had really loved me, he wouldn't have done it. He would have shared with me whatever was going on in his mind. He said I was the most important thing in his life. We knew each other forever. We were going to be together forever. If it was enough for me, why wasn't it enough for him? So why leave the most important thing in your life?" And then I said, "Now both of us don't have anyone to love, right, Mama?" I knew it was spiteful, but I couldn't help myself.

Mama looked away for a minute. When she turned around, I saw tears in her eyes.

"You are a dear foolish sixteen. There is so much left for you to understand."

I waited. "What?"

"You, your babushka, and I are . . . so alike. We all fell head over heels in love."

"Babushka?"

"Yes, Babushka."

"She's never told me about falling in love."

"It was long ago, and she's a clever lady."

"But Mama, what is clever about hiding stories? She knows I love her."

"She knows you need to tell her *your* story, so she listens and doesn't talk about herself."

"Was it your papa she fell in love with or was there someone else?"

"Yes, it was my father, your grandfather. She ran away with him even though her parents forbade the relationship. She was your age, sixteen. He was twenty-six, my father. And I was eight when he died."

"How did Babushka manage?"

"Well, those were hard years—no medicines, not enough doctors. After he died, she pampered me. I was her golden child. As I got older, I saw her sacrifices. With her ten fingers she cleaned streets, cleaned people's houses, scavenged for food. And we survived. Everything I am today I owe to her. Maybe I was too spoiled for Papa."

I said nothing. How could my hard-working mother ever be too spoiled?

"You were smart and beautiful, Mama. You were first in mathematics and you were gorgeous. Why wouldn't Papa fall in love with you? So what if he was a brilliant physicist?"

"He was very charming, Verushka. He'd sit on the sofa in the living room and chat with Babushka as if he had all the time in the world. And he made her laugh like I hadn't heard her laugh in years." She looked down at her hands. She touched the finger where she'd worn her wedding band. "Once, we were inseparable."

"Like Sergei and me."

"Yes. I remember when your papa was waiting to hear about his doctoral studies. Nothing was more important to him than being accepted for his advanced studies—nothing, not even me."

"So what are you saying? That Sergei's sui—what Sergei did to himself was more important to him than I was?"

"No, no, that's not what I'm saying. But he had a secret world that he was afraid to tell you about, or just couldn't. And your papa also had his private world, his secrets and his own ambitions. I wasn't part of that world. Your Papa could spend hours with people who he thought would help advance his career, people I never met."

And I remembered the afternoons when Sergei would sit with me on a bench under the trees of Primorsky Boulevard, holding me, but I would feel he was a million miles away. Or the evenings with friends when I would see a black cloud cross his face and he would become silent.

"Are you sorry you married him, Mama?"

"No, I loved him. When he was accepted for his doctoral studies and received a lecturer's position on the faculty, we decided to get married. I thought no matter what happens, what he does, the time with him will be worth any pain."

"Will I feel the same about my pain?"

"I don't know, little sparrow. I hope so. It's better than anger."

"When did you find out Papa was Jewish?"

"We were not married as Jews—we were married in city hall by a clerk. That was the first and last time I ever met his parents."

"My grandparents?"

"Yes. It was his mother who told me their name had been Brodsky."

"How could you love him, after he lied to you?"

"Verushka, love is strange. It has as many variations as a violin concerto. Papa is brilliant and fascinating, he can charm the birds off a tree. I didn't think not telling me was a lie—I thought it was fear, protecting me from harm. He was afraid and *is* afraid, truly afraid of what tomorrow may bring. Maybe because he saw how his own father suffered. I don't know. When you get older, you get more frightened."

I said nothing to Irena about any of this. Irena had loved Sergei like a brother and she adored Papa. After all, at twelve she was too young to help me, or to share my pain and anger. If Grandfather Brodsky could survive the gulag, I surely could travel on my own to Israel and make a new life.

I put Sergei's pictures into my suitcase together with all of his notes and birthday cards I'd saved. I'd take him with me to Israel.

The traffic narrows into a single lane. Ahead of us is the airport entrance. Each vehicle is being directed to pass through a series of roadblocks. We slow down to a crawl. Suddenly the bus driver brakes sharply. Ahead of us a gray-and-white van has been stopped. I slide the bus window open and watch. A Border Patrol soldier wearing a thick padded vest and carrying an M-16 orders the van's driver out. He motions to the driver to open the back of the van. Another soldier walks over. The three go to the back. They don't exchange a word. The first soldier opens the back of the van and stands a careful few feet from the door. He watches while the other two soldiers poke at each of the tires and at a pile of packages. I look at the expression on his face. I feel sorry for the driver. I remember standing in front of the passport man at the Odessa airport. I felt like a bug then.

But there is no reaction on the driver's face. I see his foot tapping the asphalt. Is it nervousness, does he have something to hide? A bomb? In the rear of the van, next to the bundles and packages, a heavily robed Arab woman stares out at the soldiers. She rocks a wailing baby who probably was wakened by the sudden stop. The soldiers ignore the mother and child. Still no one says anything, not a single word. The skinny soldier, the one who looks the youngest, slams the rear door shut. The other two soldiers gesture to the Arab, meaning that he can get back into the van and continue on his way into the airport.

The driver quickly climbs in and starts the engine. The tallest soldier walks into the low building near the checkpoint. His rifle knocks against the pot of geraniums near the door. I will remember to tell Baruch that the checkpoint has flowers even though it might be blown up.

The bus driver presses on the door lever and it swings open. The skinny soldier pokes his head in, looks around, and gives a thumbs-up signal—*"B'seder, habibi."* It's okay, buddy.

I leave my window open. The warm breeze feels pleasant.

9:35 AM **Baruch Ben Tov** Kibbutz Broshim, Judean Hills

My hand tamps down the moist soil. The radio is playing the last movement of Beethoven's Ninth. I am potting fifty geranium cuttings. Will this work be as enjoyable for Thomas Wanninger, high school student from Berlin, as it is for me? On his application he checked off working in the gardens as his first choice, then the cow sheds. Odd—first time a teenage boy coming here has wanted to work with plants and flowers.

Vera's nervous about being his kibbutz buddy. It's the first time she's been assigned a teenage boy—I think that's what's making her unsure of herself. I told her she'll be fine. She's never failed at any task.

I usually get some help from volunteers with the mowing and weeding. Volunteers like working with the tractors, the irrigation equipment, even paving and fence repair. I've never had a volunteer who was interested in potting or learning how to graft plants. Thomas also made a particular request to go to Jerusalem. Maybe he is a religious boy, interested in the churches there and the holy sites.

Of course, Vera is special. She wants to be a botanist. She

seems to get something very personal out of nurturing plants and flowers. There's so much she can teach this boy.

In the three years she has been here she has become like a granddaughter to me. I call her my princess. She reminds me of no one in my past, and that is a relief to me. There is something regal about her walk, the way she tilts her head—like a princess listening to her subjects. She is blond, slim, tall enough to reach with ease all the shelves in the garden sheds. She is a very happy person, but suddenly like a passing cloud covering the sun, she becomes sad. I ask her what is the matter, but she always answers, "Nothing." This year she has told me more. About Odessa and her family, and about a boy called Sergei. Someone she loved but who didn't come to Israel. She hasn't explained why. Maybe now that she has Dan, she is more willing to talk.

I say nothing about my past to her, but then no one dares to ask, not even Vera. Everyone in the kibbutz steps around my history as if it is a plot of scorched earth, not to be trodden on.

A few months ago she said, "I want you to know something, Baruch. My father's name is Alex Ushakov. It's not Brodsky. If he ever writes to you, asking about me, don't answer him. Don't write a word."

"How would he know about me?"

"He's probably bribed my little sister to show him my letters."

I was shocked by what she told me and by the look of fierce determination on her face.

"Do you promise, Baruch?"

"Yes," I said.

The Beethoven symphony ends. The beeping time signal sounds. "Good morning. This is the ten-o'clock news." I look at my watch. Yes, ten o'clock already.

"Last night extra security measures were taken in the Jerusalem area, amid urgent warnings of pending terror attacks.

Police have increased surveillance and have apprehended and questioned illegal Palestinian workers. Checks are being made on all stolen vehicles to prevent their use as car bombs. Yesterday a bomb exploded next to a bus traveling on the Haifa–Tel Aviv highway. The bus was damaged, but no one was injured.

"The weather for today will be hot in all parts of the country, with increased humidity in the coastal areas. The next scheduled news broadcast is at eleven o'clock. We continue with our program of classical music."

No reason to worry. It's not her first time picking up a volunteer. She is very mature for her nineteen years, and she is on the direct bus to the airport, with only one stop. She's a sensible girl who doesn't panic.

From the airport to the kibbutz she and the German boy, this Thomas Wanninger, will be traveling on Highway 1, nowhere near the center of Jerusalem. No danger.

I hear the first notes of a Mozart piano concerto; I turn up the volume and hum along. I am nearly finished with the geranium cuttings.

10:30 AM Thomas Wanninger El Al flight 01: SXF–TLV (Berlin–Tel Aviv)

I am about to be a total stranger in a strange land. The plane moves over the coast of Israel. The Mediterranean is a deep blue with patches of shallow green water near the shore. I'm surprised by the skyscrapers of Tel Aviv—why did I think there would be desert and camels? We fly over Tel Aviv and now there are farms, small red-roofed houses, and palm trees. We are told to fasten seat belts, seats in an upright position, get ready for landing. The local time is 10:30 A.M., the temperature is thirty degrees centigrade. No more rain, fog, overcoats, or umbrellas, Tommi, I say to myself. I grin.

"First visit to Israel?" the flight attendant asks.

"Yes."

"Well, have a good time."

Walking down the steps from the plane, a wave of the old fear crashes over me. The feeling I used to have when I went to the hospital to see my father. Being afraid he would die in front of me. Walking down the hospital corridor, breathing as if I'd run a hundred kilometers. Now I feel it again. What the hell am I doing here? On my own? I could get killed here. Who has time to care about a German kid in this country? Coming here was a mistake. And I won't find out anything.

The glare of the sun makes me blink and I feel the heat of it on the back of my neck. I almost trip. My feet are beginning to sweat in my hiking boots. I should have worn sandals. Thomas Wanninger, exile from another planet. I take my sweatshirt off. I see a guy grinning at my T-shirt.

"Hey, great to have another soccer fan in Israel. Your favorite team?" he says, looking at the logo on my T-shirt. He speaks English with an accent. Maybe he's Israeli.

"Yes, Arminia-Berlin," I say.

"I hope they're winners, buddy. Have a good time here. *Shalom.*" He smiles and strolls away. He has no luggage, so I guess he's Israeli. I feel better. It's got to be okay here if they know about soccer.

"Will someone be waiting for you at the arrivals terminal?" It's a woman in an airport uniform.

"Yes, I'm going to a kibbutz. There'll be someone from the kibbutz."

"I'm the ground stewardess." She smiles. "After you pick up your luggage, you go out that way." She points to a green arrow.

I take the instruction sheet out of my jeans pocket and look at the name again—Vera Brodsky.

There have been two ambushes, one from the side of the road, the other on the outskirts of a settlement. Three people killed, two injured. One of them a guy I knew. He got it from a sniper.

Our leave is canceled. I couldn't get hold of Vera to let her know. Left a message on my dad's cell phone.

Well, that's the way it is in the army. The only certain thing is that nothing's certain. So, I'm in my combat fatigues and ready to go.

In the back of the jeep no one's talking. We're thinking about tomorrow, next year—not today. That's the way we get through today. We pass a cluster of villages with silvery green olive groves, women hanging laundry, and goats grazing. Who knows what might be under those fields: Roman forts, Byzantine mosaics, Paleolithic tools, all waiting to be uncovered by archaeologists. Maybe I'll be the lucky archaeologist. My university application is in. Vera still has to make up her mind.

The jeep leaves the highway. Touching the flat fields is a straight line of blue sky. As blue as Vera's eyes. My beautiful Vera.

"It's those two houses down the road."

"Do we surround or go in, Sergeant?" I ask.

"Go in and get everybody out."

"Women and children?"

"Yes, everybody. We have to search."

Seven of us walk down the dirt street. Carefully. My feet are sweating; there must be pools of water in my boots. Trying to see clearly in the harsh sunlight, I aim my M-16 from left to right, then from right to left, like a metronome. Someone has been baking *pitot* on a *taboun* at the entrance to a half-empty grocery store. I'm hungry, and the smell of fresh bread is tempting, but we continue to move toward the hill. Our olive-drab uniforms blend in with the dust.

The sandbagged armored personnel carrier has followed us and waits at the top of the hill with the engine running. If people were out on this village street, they're gone now. Whoever was hanging laundry has left a shirt on the line dangling like a one-armed man. The children who were playing dropped their ball maybe seconds ago, because it is still rolling. The houses are shut tight, but I know we're being watched. Zebedeid looks deserted, but all of us know it isn't.

We head for the first of the two houses. No one's talking. The sergeant kicks his boot against the pale blue metal door.

"*Iftach!*" he shouts. "Open up!"

His command echoes up and down the road. The door opens slightly, and I see the head and shoulders of a woman.

"Where is your son Sameh?" the sergeant asks. He leans on the door. The woman backs away. The door swings open.

Vera Brodsky Arrivals terminal, Ben Gurion Airport   10:30 AM

A man is coming out of the double doors pushing a cart with two suitcases balanced on it. Funny how much he looks like my father. What a joke, my father coming to see me. *I miss you, Verushka. Come back home.*

The man comes closer—no, just an ordinary man who does not look anything like my father. I hold the cardboard sign above my head: THOMAS WANNINGER.

Dan Oron Israel Army patrol, Zebedeid, Palestinian Authority   10:45 AM

"What's going on in there? Over."

It's the officer in the armored personnel carrier. I answer.

"Receiving. Here, nothing. None of the other kids are home, only the mother. Sameh is gone. The mother knows nothing. She's not talking. She swears she hasn't seen him for more than a week. He's a good boy and Omar's a good boy. Doesn't know where her son is. Her answers don't tell us anything except Omar's his buddy. Over."

We back out of the cinder-block house. The metal door clangs shut behind us, but we can hear the woman weeping. It's more like wailing. My uniform is sticking to my body, we're all stinking from sweat. The flies are buzzing around our faces. My lips feel cracked. I wipe my sleeve across them. This isn't the place or the time to stop and open my water canteen.

The sun throws our shadows onto a concrete wall with slogans in Arabic spray-painted on it in red and black: *Yahud*—Jew, us. Portraits of two suicide bombers have been painted above the slogans, young guys from this village who blew themselves up and are now the martyrs of Zebedeid.

For us, death isn't just a slogan, it's immediate. We keep moving, no talking, our M-16s shifting from side to side. It's hot. I can't believe how dry my mouth is or the stink that's coming from my body. Even Vera wouldn't love me now. My equipment is sticking to me like glue. None of us wants to die. Not here, not now. We move carefully. No one says anything, there's nothing to say, we've done this enough times. Without speaking, we move toward the second house. We surround it.

"Iftach!"—Open up!

An old man opens the wooden door and shouts, "No one is here!" He is holding a birdcage. The two canaries in the cage flutter up and down. They peck at the bars and make squeaking sounds. Three of us brush past the old man and enter. He shrugs his shoulders and sits down on a rusty kitchen chair.

We start overturning the furniture, what there is of it. I'm slamming drawers open and shut, but there are no pistols, no suspicious wires or timers that can be used for putting bombs together. I turn around and look at the old man. He looks back at me and then shuts his eyes.

The sergeant motions us to leave. The soldiers surrounding

the house gather in front. I give the signal to the armored personnel carrier to move back down the hill.

Vera Brodsky Arrivals terminal, Ben Gurion Airport   11:00 AM

I'm sure the tall kid with the white T-shirt, the washed-out jeans, the heavy boots is Thomas Wanninger even though he doesn't look very German. His hair is dark and curly. There's something about him that's almost Jewish. He probably wouldn't like someone saying that. I'm wearing a pair of jeans, the same as he is. I've got a T-shirt on and so does he. I'm nineteen, he's sixteen, three years younger than me, but I feel a hundred years older than he. I'm part of the landscape, he's a stranger.

I hold the sign above my head. He spots me and waves. He does not bother with a cart—he's carrying his suitcase.

Thomas Wanninger Arrivals terminal, Ben Gurion Airport   11:00 AM

I see a girl waving a sign with my name. The terminal is crowded with people. It amazes me. Why did I think everyone in this country would be behind locked doors, stuck in their houses, afraid to come out into the open? This isn't what I expected, nothing like what I've seen on the TV news reports. Everyone looks relaxed, people are laughing, kissing and hugging visitors, like a terminal where people have arrived for a vacation trip. Mutti was so worried about nothing.

There are masses of people ahead of me surging out of the baggage claim area. The line crawls slowly toward the waiting area. I have time to look at all the shops. I can't believe how many have signs in English: ICE CREAM, MONEY CHANGED, RENT-A-CAR, FRESH FLOWERS. I walk toward the tall blond girl. She doesn't look much older than me, maybe nineteen or twenty. I don't know why, but I was expecting someone older, like a teacher or a guide.

I'm sweating from the effort of not hitting someone with my suitcase. The terminal is packed, trying to get out is like moving through glue, the pushing and shoving is in a million languages: "Excuse me." "Sorry." "Where's the exit?" It's like a party everyone wants to get to. No one's mad. It will take me at least five minutes to get to where she is standing.

People waving, people in sandals, babies in strollers, dogs yipping around their owners' feet, so normal, everything so normal. Amazing.

"Hi, I'm Thomas Wanninger," and then I laugh. "Of course you know that." Vera is pretty, really pretty, and blonder than Christina with eyes bluer than Christina's. There is no way she matches Christina's image of a Jewish girl. Ha! I will have to remember this moment.

11:05 AM **Vera Brodsky** Arrivals terminal, Ben Gurion Airport

I see the relief on his face. I know what he was thinking. It's normal, it's an airport like any other airport, anyplace in the world. He must have been scared to come here. I wonder how he got his mother to give her permission. No father, no brothers or sisters— it probably was pretty hard for him to convince her. What was it that pushed him to come here, in the middle of an *intifada,* with Palestinians and Israelis being injured and killed almost every day?

"*Shalom,* Thomas, I'm Vera Brodsky. You have my name on your travel sheet." When I say my name, I feel the way Babushka promised me I would—strong and independent—all over again. Funny that the feeling is so strong today, after more than three years. And with this German kid. It's a beautiful spring day and I am going to take care of Thomas Wanninger, because people trust me and know I can do it.

"I hope your suitcase isn't too heavy, because we're going to have to run for the bus. Our station is at the other end of the terminal, outside, near the entrance."

He nods. "No problem. My legs are pretty long."

"Good. Mine, too."

We laugh and start to cut our way through the crowds of people. "If we miss it, then there's an hour and a half to wait before the next bus. This one is direct, with only two stops before Jerusalem. The first one is a diner where the bus stops for drinks and the toilet facilities and to pick up soldiers going to Jerusalem. The stop after that is Broshim."

Thomas Wanninger Ben Gurion Airport   11:07 AM

We are both running, and she is shouting the explanation above the noise of the crowd in the terminal. Then we are outside, half walking fast, half running, along the sidewalk. She has her hair in a long braid and wears big silver hoop earrings. Christina has a pair like that—she calls them Gypsy earrings.

"How do I pay for the bus, Vera? I don't have any Israeli money."

"Don't worry about it. I have enough for both of us."

"I'll pay you back when I change my money," I say.

"It's not my money—it's the kibbutz that's paying."

"So what do I do to repay it?"

"Oh, work for about five hundred hours," she says, and grins at me.

"Slave labor, is that it?" I say, grinning back at her.

"Right. There's the bus, at the stop, run."

We both run toward the bus. I can see the driver motioning with his hand for us to slow down. He will wait.

Vera Brodsky Number 9 bus from Ben Gurion Airport to   11:08 AM
Jerusalem

Good thing Thomas knows how to run, even though I see the bus driver signaling that he will wait for us. We're the last people to get on the bus. Thomas starts to move to the back. I can see there aren't two seats together at the rear. I point to two empty seats in the second row, at the front of the bus, on the right-hand side. He sits down while I take money out to pay for the bus tickets.

10:08 AM Ilse Wanninger Aachener Strasse 366, Berlin

(BERLIN TIME)

"*Guten* . . . excuse me . . . Good day, is this the kibbutz, Kibbutz Broshim? . . . I'm sorry. . . . I'll speak louder, this is not a good connection. I want to talk to a German student who is working at the kibbutz. . . . His name is Thomas Wanninger. . . . Today. . . . Oh, I see. . . . Of course. At least half an hour? . . . Is it possible to leave a message? . . . Thank you. Could you tell him his mother called to say she was leaving Berlin for a few days? Going to Augsburg. *Danke.* Thank you. *Wiederhören.* And tell him I'll call when I return home. Goodbye."

11:08 AM Sameh Laham Yoni's Diner, Highway 1

Today the Boss is featuring stuffed cabbage and hamburgers in the diner. There's a high stack of pots and pans in the kitchen; the sink is clogged with meat scraps. The Boss leans against the swinging kitchen door.

"Everything all right, Sameh? Your mother feeling better? You won't take any more time off?" The Boss doesn't wait for my answer. I'm here to clean, wipe up, carry, not to have a conversation with him.

"Next week, Sameh, next week it will all be over. My boy, my Yoni, will be safe. Things are getting better, Sameh. A party, that's what I'm going to have. Right here, a real party. Too bad we can't get your mother past the barricades. She'd prepare a real *hafla,* wouldn't she? You people know how to make those stuffed vine leaves, the *makluba,* all those dishes.

"My Yoni, finally finishing his army service. I can't believe it.

Three years and thank God not a scratch on him—not shot in an ambush, not stoned in one of those terrorist villages. Just a beard he's trying to grow." He laughs, my boss. Since this morning he can't stop talking—he's in a good mood today. So am I. I'm going to be out of this shit situation, this war, this occupation.

The Boss is always mentioning my mother, how she cooks, what she cooks, but he doesn't even know her. He thinks when "peace" comes, I'll be cleaning his toilets and my mother will be cooking in his kitchen.

My mother is up at five. She doesn't need a clock, because Rifat Jabari's rooster, in the yard of the house behind ours, has been crowing for at least a half hour. When she's put the kettle on, she wakes up my brothers. They grumble, they moan, they yawn, but they get dressed, and then she gives each a glass of mint tea. She doesn't let any of them sit at the table and dream. They must be out of the house and on their way, avoiding army searches for Palestinian kids on the roads around Israeli towns.

The four of them walk from village to village with plastic bags on their backs or balanced on their heads. The bags are filled with T-shirts, girls' dresses, sets of forks and knives. They drink water from the fountains of mosques, they rest in the shade of pine trees, they open their bags on dirty sidewalks near traffic lights and fruit stands. They walk and walk and walk. A lucky day is when they can sneak into an Israeli village, near a market or gas station, and sell something to a passerby looking for a bargain. At night they come back home. Sometimes they have a few Israeli shekels to give my mother.

And my boss is waiting for peace and for my mother to come to the diner and cook for him. My mother has forgotten how to cook meat or chicken. She has not cooked those in a year. But tomorrow she will have them.

The man who owns this van is an English soccer fan—there's a Manchester United pennant on the front seat. I'm also a Manchester United fan. That doesn't make this Israeli and me friends. You can't be friends with someone stupid, so stupid he leaves the keys in his car. Because he owns the garage, he thinks his van won't be stolen. I know all about him, this Roni Abulafia, because I've been watching him and his garage, and his workers, and his children. Even when the police pulled me in to question me, I managed to come back here. You see, I'm smart. We talk about soccer, and once he told me to stick around because the best goalkeeper in Israel was coming in to have his Volvo tuned up. "He'll give you an autograph, Omar. I'll tell him to."

I sleep in Mr. Roni's car wash, in the back, so easy, so simple. Today there will be a big surprise for Mr. Israeli Owner of a Garage. Oh, what a surprise. If I had the time, if I wanted to, I could show this Jew how I play soccer. Me, from Jabel Fahm, I'm good enough for any team in Europe. Who cares now about being a soccer star? There's more to life than soccer, or garages, or a brand-new shiny van. Life is about showing the world our land will not be occupied.

Abulafia is always saying how worried he is, taxes, his kids' teeth need braces, his father is getting old. "Worries, worries, Omar. But you're young, you have no worries, a big plate of hummus, a pack of cigarettes, a couple of shekels in your pocket, and life is simple."

He's right, a person like me has no worries. Because I have plans for the future. My only worry is Sameh. Sameh is weak, he's too emotional, he gets tears in his eyes when he talks about his mother and his brothers and sisters. I worry about how tough Sameh is—how strong his belief is.

He's fallen asleep. His head and shoulder are leaning against the bus window. He told me he was up at three o'clock this morning. His mother drove him to the airport. He lives forty minutes from the airport with his mother.

We put his suitcase in a space near the rear door of the bus. His backpack is on his lap, one hand holding the straps. I unzip my straw bag and take out a book about desert vegetation that Baruch gave me. Then I put it back and take out a pad and my pen instead. I'll write a letter to Dan, to his army P.O.B. Then a letter to "the ladies," as Mama calls herself, Babushka, and Irena. A house without Papa. I'll let Thomas sleep until the bus makes its stop at the highway diner.

Lidia and I talked last night about being a buddy to boy volunteers. For the past two years I've been a buddy to two American girls and a girl from Birmingham, England. I've never been the SEEK buddy of a boy. But because this German kid wants to work in the gardens, I've been given the assignment. He says he's interested in botany.

I told Lidia I was worried about how Thomas would react to Baruch. I can't stand the idea of someone asking Baruch questions or staring at the number on his arm. "After all, Lidia, he *is* German." She says I'm better off saying nothing. "You don't know how much he learned about the Holocaust, what his feelings are." Let the kid come to his own conclusions, and Baruch will also handle it in his own way. If there's a problem, well, Lidia was sure the kibbutz would switch him to something else or he would go home earlier. These German kids know what they're in for, Lidia says. It's part of why they come to Israel.

I look at Thomas sleeping. Does he know he's going to work with a man as old as Baruch? A man who could be his grandfather? Baruch looks like the prophet of doom in Babushka's illustrated Bible. He is tall, and he doesn't have the stoop of old age. He has dark lines under his eyes. His thick white hair curls up from his head as if his mind is on fire. He lives alone in a small house on the edge of the sunflower field.

It doesn't matter if he's worked in the fields or in the nursery—when I come for tea in the afternoon, he is in a spotless shirt, ironed like a holiday tablecloth, and pants that have creases as straight as a ruler. He pours tea for me, and his hands are immaculate and the nails perfectly trimmed. Baruch's shirts are short sleeved. Thomas will certainly see the numbers.

11:20 AM **Sameh Laham** Yoni's Diner, Highway 1

Sunday—the diner is crowded. Soldiers on their way to army bases, soldiers on their way home for leave, truck drivers, bus passengers wanting a quick cold drink or to use the bathroom, people on their way to Jerusalem, kids on a school trip, yeah, the Boss is glad I am back this morning.

"Saved my life, Sameh, can't imagine getting through another day without you. Damn lucky you're a *gingee*—they don't spot you as an Arab so fast."

My father had red hair, that's who I get it from. My brothers and sisters have my mother's dark curly hair. Omar used to say I could play for an Irish soccer team. "Don't you know, Sameh, all the Irish have red hair!"

The man said: "Sameh, take care, remember Allah, repeat the verses from the Koran, pay attention to everything you see, concentrate on the task ahead. Be strong, my friend, in this, your first battle." This is what the man said to me, the man in the small room. I memorized eight verses, the verses about a *shaheed*. The verses became as much a part of me as my heartbeat. The words of every verse promised me paradise, because I will die a true martyr.

I started to think about it in December. Four months ago, on a Friday, after the prayers in the mosque, Omar took me to meet the man. We walked for two hours. Along the way I told myself I was sure to be accepted immediately. We came to a house. One wall was painted blue, and the other three walls were raw cinderblocks. Omar knocked. An old woman opened the metal door. She looked at us suspiciously, but Omar whispered something and she opened the door wide enough to let us in.

We followed the old woman down a hallway. The house was as long and as narrow as an alley. She opened a door and we entered a small room. There was no furniture in the room except a prayer rug, a table, and a chair.

On the table was the Koran and an automatic rifle—a Kalashnikov. On the seat of the chair was a video camera.

A man in a dark green shirt and pants, like a uniform, with a *keffiyeh* covering his head and face, was sitting cross-legged on the rug. All I could see of his face was his eyes. He looked up at us. He nodded to Omar. Omar pushed me forward. "Tell him, Sameh," he said.

I told the man my story: my father's cancer, my mother not being able to feed my brothers and sisters, my brothers peddling, none of us in school anymore. On the wall, above the table, was a picture of the Al Aqsa Mosque. There was also a clock on the wall. I spoke quickly. I said to myself, This man has more important things to do than listen to a sixteen-year-old boy. So as I spoke, I kept my eyes fixed on the golden dome of the holy mosque and on the moving minute hand of the clock. It didn't take more than five minutes for me to tell him about myself. Five minutes—that was all—for my whole life.

Outside, I heard the bell of the water truck and then the opening of doors. I heard women chattering and the banging of pails and containers as they waited to fill up, to get their supply of water.

The man said nothing. He stared at his hands. What was he

thinking? Then he looked up and asked me where I worked, and when I told him at the diner outside Jerusalem on Highway 1, he looked at me, looked into my eyes, for the first time since I'd entered the room. But he didn't say I was accepted for the task. In a low voice, very slowly, he said, "Go home, Sameh, go back to Zebedeid, go back to your Israeli boss, think very hard about this. If you are sure, come back in a month. Omar will know where to find me."

I stood outside the house and waited for Omar. The old woman swept the three steps below the door; they weren't more than loose bricks, one stuck on top of the other. She swept around my feet and then went inside. I was sure Omar was telling the man I could be trusted.

"Bring your stuff, Sameh?"

"Yes, Boss."

"Put it in the broom closet?"

"Yes, Boss."

"Okay, back to work. One week is a helluva lot of dirty dishes and stinking floors. Lots for you to do."

11:30 AM Vera Brodsky Number 9 bus from Ben Gurion Airport to Jerusalem

Looking down the road, I can see the yellow-and-red sign on the low roof of the diner: YONI'S DINER * FRESH FOOD * QUICK SERVICE. Two more minutes before the bus reaches the diner and pulls in. I shake Thomas's shoulder.

He opens his eyes and looks at me. I can see he is confused. *"Ja, was ist los?"*

"Thomas, it's okay. You fell asleep."

"Oh, sorry, Vera. Forgot for a minute where I am."

"You slept through a lot of beeping horns and traffic jams. You must be dead tired."

He grins at me. "Good thing I didn't start calling you *Dummkopf* for waking me up. I take a seven o'clock bus to my high school. Even the driver is used to my falling asleep. I guess when you woke me, I thought you were the bus driver and I was somewhere off Linden Platz." He laughs.

I like him. He has a sense of humor about himself that is nice.

"Over there"—I point straight ahead—"you can see the diner. I'll have a chance to get us something cold to drink. Maybe you want something to eat, use the bathroom, whatever."

"Yeah, I see it. Look at all those cars. Is it packed this way every day? Must be a popular place."

"Sunday's a regular day," I explain. "Our weekend is only one day—the Sabbath. So lots of soldiers and people travel, to work, to an army base, on a Sunday. Small country—the bus is the way most of us get around. And this diner is the only place to get real food between the airport and Jerusalem. You're right—it's very popular. Everyone stops here."

"You know, I *am* hungry."

The bus pulls into the parking area at the back of the diner. The driver opens the front and rear doors.

Thomas stretches his legs, stands up, and straps his backpack on. I put my straw bag on my shoulder and we get off the bus.

Sameh Laham Yoni's Diner, Highway 1 11:41 *AM*

I can see most of the diner from the sink where I am washing, because the Boss and the two waiters keep swinging open the kitchen door to pick up the orders. There are soldiers at practically every table. The passengers from the number 9 to Jerusalem are sharing chairs or standing. Five or six regulars are leaning against the counter eating their hamburgers standing up. Kids, probably on some school trip, are joking and pushing one another around near the door. They are all bunched up by the candy counter and the ice cream freezer.

Ben, the cook, has his back to me, and the Boss is over at the cash register. The bus driver walks over to the cash register and takes out his wallet. He pays. It has to be now. I know the bus will pull out in another minute. I leave the water running in the sink and go around the half wall behind the kitchen. I open the broom closet and take out the green backpack.

11:42 AM Thomas Wanninger Yoni's Diner, Highway 1

I finish the pita and hummus Vera bought for me. "It was as good as you said it would be," I tell her. I see the bus driver get up and go to the cash register. "I think we'd better get going."

11:43 AM Sameh Laham Outside Yoni's Diner, Highway 1

My hands are still wet from the dishes, so I wipe my hair down, then wipe them dry on my pants. I am wearing one of the Boss's old T-shirts. It has Hebrew lettering on it. I look like an Israeli.

I leave the kitchen by the back door and go around through the parking lot. All the soldiers have left the diner and are lined up waiting to get on the bus. I look at their M-16s. In a few minutes nothing will help them. I tighten the shoulder strap of the backpack. I move it closer to my neck.

I stand at the end of the line, very close to the side of the bus. The soldiers are kidding around, talking to one another. The bus driver tells them to hurry up. Now there are just three soldiers ahead of me. I remember the video I recorded. Too bad there is no one to film me now, at the very minute before.

Outside, we stand in line waiting to get back on the bus. The bus driver looks at everyone carefully, as if by looking he can tell everything about them. Two Arab women, one holding a baby, one with a stuffed shoulder bag, get on. I can see paper diapers sticking out of the bag. The bus driver nods, and the women move down the aisle. Six soldiers give the driver a loud greeting in Hebrew. A group of school kids and their teacher get on next. A pregnant woman, a man with a laptop, two girls about my age, a kid carrying a basketball, a grandmother and grandfather with two grandchildren, and all the passengers who boarded the bus at Ben Gurion airport get back on.

I can see the driver staring at my backpack. Is it because I look foreign?

"Does he want me to open it?" I ask Vera.

"Don't worry about it—it's okay," Vera says to the bus driver. She says it in English, I guess so I'll understand, and then repeats it in Hebrew.

"He doesn't speak Hebrew. He's a volunteer coming to my kibbutz. We got on together at the airport. He's okay, there's nothing to worry about."

"It doesn't bother me, Vera. I'll open it." I open the backpack. The driver peers inside, feels the bottom, puts his hand in and pulls out the envelope. The envelope with the photographs.

"What's this?" he asks me in English.

"Just some photographs," I say, praying he won't take the envelope out and open it.

"Okay, *todah*. Thank you."

We both board the bus. Our two seats in the front are still empty. We sit down. I turn around. Now the bus is full. Fifty-four people waiting for the driver to start the engine.

The driver reaches for the lever to pull the door shut.

Looking up into the bus, I see the driver start to reach for the door lever. I get on as fast as I can. There are three steps; I take one, and then two at once. I keep my eyes down. On the top step I am close enough to see the black hairs on the driver's arm. I turn my body, raise my eyes, and look at everyone in the bus. In my head I start to repeat the verses, the holy verses about a martyr's entrance into Paradise.

The prayers are helping me. I feel swift and strong.

In the back, I see two women. They are sitting in the two seats near the rear door. They wear long dresses, one black, one gray, and their heads are covered like my mother's with full white scarves. What is my mother doing on this bus? "Be brave, Sameh," I whisper to myself. I can't stop looking at them. What is happening to the courage of my faith? I pay the driver. He looks at the money, glances at me, sees the T-shirt. He's in a hurry. He doesn't ask me to open my backpack. I move past the first two seats. Slowly.

One woman is rocking a baby in her arms. My mother rocked my little brother the same way. And the other woman is smiling and tickling the baby. I back up, move away. My mouth is dry. My tongue sticks to the roof of my mouth. I cannot form the words of the Koran. I am in the bus but not in the bus.

My left hand reaches up to the shoulder strap of the backpack. I let the strap slide, slip, the bag falls off my shoulder. It lands with a quiet thud. Not much noise, not enough for people to look at me. I am dizzy. Allah, watch over me.

The bus driver shouts something. Someone hits my head. My forehead crushes against my eyes. My legs shake. I do not fall. I turn my head. I see through the long glass of the front door. A yellow van is near the bus. Too close. Someone has pushed my face against the glass. Are they going to throw me out, kill me?

The bus driver beeps his horn at the yellow van. The van driver holds something large and black. He looks up at the bus. I can see his face. It is Omar. Why is Omar here?

Number 9 bus from Ben Gurion Airport to Jerusalem 11:47 AM

Explosion.

EemahElohimMuttiPapaMamaGottAbuyahAllahYaumiMom GodEemahDadMamaElohimAllahMuttiMuttiYaumiDadPapa PapaMamaMamaEemahYaumiYaumiGodGodGodElohimMom MomGottGottDadYaumiMuttiYaumiEemahEemahGottDad AllahAllahMamaMamaDadDadElohimGodAbuyahMuttiPapa EemahYaumiGottAllahEemah

Mutti

Eemah

God

Abuyah

PapaMama   *Elohim*

Yaumi

Dad

Al

11:54:05 AM **Radio newscast—Eyewitness interview Highway 1**

I saw the bus pull out of the parking lot. I was driving behind the bus. I was in the middle lane. It signaled it was moving into the middle lane. I slowed down to let it get in front of me. A yellow van came out of nowhere. Maybe it also pulled out of the diner, I don't know. It got so close to the bus, I thought it would scrape the side. Then the van and the bus blew up. In a second. It all happened in a second. The people on the bus were blown out of the windows, the seats, their bodies, shoes. It was awful.

12:01 PM **Radio newscast—Eyewitness interview Highway 1**

People got out of their cars and began running. Some people ran to the bus to help. Other people ran away, away from the bus. Maybe they thought more bombs would go off. Police cars came and also Border Patrol jeeps. I don't know how many. And ambulances. I heard ambulances. I was surprised they arrived so fast. Because of the explosion I couldn't hear anything, like I was deaf for a few minutes.

12:04 PM **Radio newscast—Live at the scene Highway 1**

The explosion ignited the fuel tank. The bus is completely gutted. Ambulances are arriving. Police quickly cordoned off the diner and two thousand meters of highway. Parts of the orange groves on both sides of the highway are blocked off. The search is on for other explosives or other bombers. Rescue crews and firemen are at work at this very grisly scene. Police dogs are sniffing the entire bus wreckage of twisted metal, seat frames, and ripped-up rubber flooring. The explosives were packed with nails, bolts, and shrapnel. The police are looking for clues that will provide information about the terrorist group responsible for the suicide attack.

Jerusalem hospitals are being updated as to the expected number of casualties and the type of injuries. The police are rerouting traffic. Drivers should call 411 for alternate routes into and out of Jerusalem.

We will be broadcasting throughout the day. The prime minister's office has scheduled an emergency cabinet meeting. So far no retaliatory military action has been taken.

In a moment we will be giving you the emergency telephone numbers. . . . Ambulances continue to arrive.

Thomas Wanninger At the scene Highway 1   *12:08:05 PM*

Why am I on the ground? Lying on the ground? I was on the bus. Sitting. Next to Vera. There's something wrong. I don't feel anything. The smell is strange. Burned. Burnt but different. I can't hear. I'm deaf. All around me pieces of glass, metal. Legs and arms touching me, pressing on me, a shoulder is in my mouth. Someone is pulling me. I think there are hundreds of people here. Kneeling, rising, falling, around me. Their shoes go past me, shoes covered in white, regular shoes.

I'm coughing and coughing. Something thick is running out of my mouth. I am being lifted, lifted.

"Deutsch. Deutsch," I say. I say this because his lips are moving but I don't know what he's saying. It was hot a while ago, wonderful hot weather. Why am I so cold? . . . I can't hear.

I want to see my body. If I see my body everything will make sense. I want to understand what has happened. Please. I want the noise to come back, sounds. I look at my left hand. I can't really move it. I'm afraid to try. It is full of holes. The skin has ripped away and there are small puddles of blood and flesh. I think I'm screaming but I only hear it in my head. My head hurts.

A man is leaning over me. He wants to help me. I see it in his eyes. He talks and stops. Waits. Wants me to answer. I have to answer. His lips are moving but I can't hear what he's saying.

"Ich kann nicht. Ich kann nicht. Bitte. Ich kann nichts hören. Bitte. Mutti. Bitte."

The man is pushing against my chest. Something is put around my neck. Up, up I go. Into. Into. It moves. The nice man is still with me here. He is doing different things to me. I want . . . I wa

12:09 pm **Paramedic radio report to Hadarim Hospital**

Victim, male, about fifteen or sixteen, talking until a minute ago, now unresponsive.

Location—one hundred meters from the Dromi junction, taking the right turn now, on the forest road. Police allowing only emergency vehicles.

12:12 pm **Paramedic radio report to Hadarim Hospital**

No victim identity, a ploni almoni. Connected to EKG machine. Being manually ventilated, cervical collar hooked in place. Visible injuries are burns to his face, penetrating wounds on hands and arms.

Pink froth coming from mouth, suspicion of massive internal bleeding. He appears to be in a deep coma. I repeat—I have checked the victim, no identification. Anonymous.

12:12 pm **Dr. Ricardo Hellman** Briefing for broadcasting and print media, Hadarim Hospital

The so-called chaos you have witnessed outside in the receiving areas is what we call "organized chaos." The number and frequency of attacks have made our response automatic and highly organized.

Some background on the types of injuries we are dealing with, which are blast injuries. This is what happened today on the number 9 bus.

The majority of the badly wounded were passengers in the rear of the bus. Bombs set off in closed areas produce burns and impact wounds, and usually penetration injuries from metal objects such as nails, bolts, and screws that were added to the explosive material. These cover the body with puncture wounds, lodge in the brain, and cause hemorrhaging in the eyes.

Our main concern is the blast wave from the explosive material that went off in the bus. We are expecting to see serious injuries to internal organs. The trauma team will deal with casualties with multiple injuries as they come into the emergency room. The slogan is ABC: airway, breathing, circulation. We can't let the blood pressure fall out of sight or the heart get erratic. We've got to stabilize the situation and we have only about sixty minutes to do it. The seconds start ticking away in the ambulance. Here, on hand to help us, are surgeons, anesthesiologists, nurses, portable x-ray machines. If we succeed, the victims have a good chance of survival.

A list of the dead and injured will be released later, as soon as families are informed. No questions at this time. Thank you.

Vera Brodsky In the bus Highway 1   12:15 pm

I am lying under a seat. A metal bar is pressing into my face. There is a shoe on my chest. A man's shoe. I can see my arm bone. There's no flesh on it. I am screaming, screaming, screaming. No one hears me. I will die. I will die. The smoke, a heavy sweet sick smell, ambulances, sirens. Don't cry, Vera. It's a waste of breath. Shout, shout. Please help me, I scream. *Ahtsteelu, Ahtsteelu.* Help.

I'm wet. Did I pee? Is it blood, my blood or someone else's? A voice above me says, "There's another one here."

"My name is Vera, my name is Vera. Please help me."

1:00 PM   **Emergency room admittance sheet, Hadarim Hospital**

Patient: Female, approx. 19 yrs. 1.68 meters. Fair complexion, blond hair, long braid, silver hoop earrings, white Nike rubber-soled shoe on right foot, jeans, pink T-shirt, butterfly tattoo on left hip. No identity papers. Anonymous. Attached: ER photo.
Preliminary Medical Report: Hair singed, facial lacerations, glass fragments, superficial cut 2 cm x 2 cm on neck. Left hand from wrist to elbow open bone fracture ulna radius. Left ankle open bleeding wound. Corner of left eye bleeding—shrapnel. Possible nerve and tendon damage from open wound. Pain extreme, possible loss of motility. No internal bleeding. Philadelphia [cervical collar] put on. Muscle torn in eye, pupils checked for head injury—O.K. / equal and reactive.
Condition: Moderate to severe.
(Seen by surgeon, orthopedist, ER nurse, ENT, opthalmologist. Temporarily placed in recovery room so patient can be stabilized and monitored until OR is free.)

1:04 PM   **Emergency room admittance sheet, Hadarim Hospital**

Patient: Male, approx. 16 yrs, 1.85 meters. Black hair, fair complexion, underpants, torn T-shirt (partial slogan—blue letters—ARMI), no shoes. No identity papers. Anonymous. Attached: ER photo.
Preliminary Medical Report: Patient in coma, GCS 2/15 [Glasgow Coma Scale]—responds to painful stimuli, groans but no verbal reaction. First to second degree burns on lower limbs. Apparent head trauma. Large deep laceration on forehead. Suspect intracranial bleed. Most probably concussion. Upper back laceration with imbedded screws, nuts, bolts in wound.
Condition: Critical.
(Seen by neurologist, surgeon, radiologist, ICU / Neurology)

"I've been a bus driver for fifteen years. I wasn't supposed to be driving today. I'm a replacement. I pulled into the parking lot of the diner. The bus was half empty from the airport. The stop at the diner picks up a lot of soldiers and people going to Jerusalem. There's a few minutes for passengers to get off and use the diner facilities or get food."

Did you get off also?

"Yes, I wanted some coffee. I made sure to lock the bus. I never take any chances. I'm one hundred percent sure the bus was locked."

How did the suicide bomber manage to get on?

"I rechecked all the passengers who got on at the airport. One foreign kid even opened his backpack for me. It wasn't hard to know who they were when they got back on after the break at the diner. The new passengers were two Arab women with a baby; a regular of mine, a nurse who works at Hadarim; the gingee, *and the rest were soldiers."*

And the bomber—

"He didn't look suspicious to me at first. He was the gingee, *you know, red hair, and his T-shirt had Hebrew lettering. He had a green backpack on his shoulder, he was a kid. He was at the end of the line."*

So you didn't think he was a Palestinian?

"No."

When did you become suspicious?

"The way he got on, real fast. Like he was in a hurry. He took the steps two at a time. It was too late to close the door. It all happened too quickly. He went right past me, down the aisle. He was talking to himself."

And then?

"My guts told me something was wrong."

What did you do?

"I tried to pull into the middle lane, but there was a yellow van blocking me. I shouted to everyone in the bus, 'M'khabel!' One of the soldiers got behind him and hit him on the head with his rifle butt."

You were still driving?

"Yes. I was trying to get around the yellow van. I saw he didn't fall. That's when he must have pulled the switch and set off the explosives in the backpack."

And then?

"Then? Well, after that I don't remember anything. Maybe I lost consciousness or something. Then I felt someone pulling me out."

What are your injuries?

"My hands and my back are burned, that's all. It's a miracle. I don't know why, but it's a miracle."

Do you know what happened to the passengers?

"No. When they pulled me out, I saw bodies and blood. It was awful. I had my ticket dispenser in my hand. Can you imagine that? Then I was in the ambulance. That's all I know."

This is the second time, isn't it, that you've been injured in a bus attack?

"Yes, I was the driver of a bus in Beersheba in 1995, when a suicide bomber got on. I guess my time's not up yet."

That was an interview with Dov Agmon, the driver of the number 9 bus, the bus blown up at 11:47 this morning by a Palestinian suicide bomber. As far as we know, the driver is the only person not seriously injured. We are waiting for Dr. Ricardo Hellman, here at Hadarim Hospital, to give us a full report.

For listeners who have just tuned in, a recap of the events so far: At approximately 11:47 this morning, the number 9 bus, traveling from Ben Gurion Airport to Jerusalem, exploded. Police assume it was a suicide bomber. Bomb squad estimations are that the bomber was carrying approximately sixteen kilograms of explosives.

The number 9 bus makes two stops before reaching Jerusalem. One is at Yoni's Diner, where it picks up soldiers and civilians. The diner is a popular eating place for travelers on Highway 1. The second stop is at Kibbutz Broshim. The explosion occurred seven hundred meters from the diner, in the middle lane of Highway 1. Fifty-four passengers and the driver were on the bus at the time of the explosion. Police have verified that passengers were killed in the explosion. No names of the dead or injured have been released. No terrorist group has claimed responsibility for the attack, and the identity of the suicide bomber is unknown.

For people seeking information, two emergency hotlines are open—the Jerusalem Municipality and Hadarim Hospital.

Emergency room admittance sheet, Hadarim Hospital   1:48 PM

Patient: Male, approx. 16 yrs. 1.62 meters. Red hair, pale olive complexion, underpants, one thong sandal. Visible scar above right eye. No identity papers. Anonymous. Attached: ER photo.
Police suspect illegal worker, Palestinian territories
Preliminary medical report: Singed hair, head & legs. Lacerations on hands, face. Abdominal area hard and distended. Conscious. Blood pressure low (80/50)—pulse 130. Patient in shock, transferred to OR. Laceration of liver—bleeding stopped and repaired. Check for further bleeding, 24 hrs. ICU. If stable, transfer to surgical ward, isolation.
Under police guard
Condition: Severe to critical.

Radio newscast—paramedic Clara Millman   2:15 PM

I'm a biology major, third year, at the university. I was studying for an exam. I haven't been a responder for long, but still I didn't expect anything to happen midmorning. The bombers usually like the morning rush hour. My pager buzzed—the message was "Bus bombing, Yoni's Diner."

Everyone knows where the diner is. From the center of Jerusalem the ambulance got there within minutes. I think there were more than fifty of us who arrived at the scene.

The road, a really big section of it, was littered with metal, glass, plastic bus upholstery. The bus was a twisted skeleton, no windows, most of the roof gone. I always think what a miracle it is that people survive. There were pieces of clothing, shirts, socks, a bra, jackets, men's belts. There were notebooks, envelopes, phones, a CD player. Some of the things had pieces of flesh stuck on them from the force of the explosion. Everybody's life and death was on the ground, on the side of the road, even in the field off the road. I saw body parts.

I treated a girl who'd been pulled out from under a bus seat. She kept asking me if she was alive. One of the policemen helped me get her into the ambulance. She'll be okay, I'm pretty sure.

What stays with me? Well, the smell. I can't define it, but once you've smelled it, you'll never get it out of your head. Awful, really awful.

3:00 PM **Lidia Adler** Waiting area, emergency room, Hadarim Hospital

I'm ice-cold. I'm scared stiff. I'm standing at the end of the corridor. Baruch is talking to the social worker. I think we might go in to see Vera. There are so many people, there's no air to breathe. I can't believe this has happened. This is something that you see on television—it's a photograph in the newspaper. This does not *ever* happen to people you know. Not to Vera, my best friend.

People are crying, huddled in corners, hugging one another. I didn't have any luck calling Dan's army base. If my father sees this on the TV news in Argentina, he'll be hysterical. He's got a map of Jerusalem and the outskirts tacked up on the kitchen wall. He knows I'm always catching a bus to go somewhere. People around me don't stop crying. Everyone seems to have a cell phone glued to his ear. What a weird mixture of kids, parents, reporters, and religious people moving their bodies in prayer. I can't hear myself think, but I'm only thinking one thing: *Please be alive, Vera, please.*

We're all sure Vera was one of the unidentified injured who were taken off the bus. There have been no calls on the SEEK line at the kibbutz. No call from Vera or the German boy. But she got to the airport okay, otherwise she would have let someone know. And if this kid hadn't seen her, he would have called the kibbutz. He had the phone number on his travel instruction sheet. No, for sure, she picked him up and they both got on the bus. *The* bus. The one that exploded. The bus traveling from Ben Gurion Airport, the bus that picks up and drops off passengers at the entrance gate of Kibbutz Broshim.

It is the only reason we can think of to explain why she and the volunteer haven't arrived at the kibbutz. Only the explosion can explain their disappearance. That's why we're here.

Vera was the first person I met when I came to Kibbutz Broshim. She'd arrived six months before and was sure she was staying. We were both sixteen. We both came to Israel without our parents. She was luckier than me—both her parents were alive. Of course, she let me know really fast that she didn't consider her father alive. He'd cheated on her mother, left the family, and moved in with another woman, and didn't want anyone to know he was Jewish. "So for me, Lidia, he's as good as dead."

She became my kibbutz buddy. We liked each other right away. Strange, because we're so different. Almost opposites, I'd say. She's serious, I'm a clown, she's blond, I'm dark, her father left home, my mother died. Vera wants to become a scientist, a botanist, and I want to be an artist, a painter or a photographer.

For both of us being in Israel, being at Broshim, was a dream come true. Here Vera didn't have to worry about skinheads, or anti-Semites, or being called *Zhid* by jealous classmates. "I can do anything I want," she kept saying over and over again. We both wanted to start a new life, become something, be part of the life at a kibbutz. It took one week for us to become best friends. And she didn't forget me when she met Dan. She kept bothering him to fix me up with this guy or that guy in his unit. All she wants for me is to be as happy as she is.

My father runs a small grocery store in Buenos Aires, and he just about scrapes by, making enough to support me and my younger brother. Art schools are expensive in Argentina. Where would I get money for school fees, for food, for equipment? It was impossible.

And then a friend's brother came back from a trip to Israel. He was working as a furniture designer on a kibbutz. Not every kibbutz is agricultural, he said. You can be almost anything. He gave me some addresses, and I started to write letters. That's how I got to Kibbutz Broshim. Maybe people living and working together like one family would make up for the emptiness in me since my mother died. My father cried, my aunts and uncles tried to persuade me to stay home, but finally everyone gave their approval and helped pay for the airplane ticket. And maybe, just maybe, I thought, I might get into an art school in Israel.

Baruch is motioning to me. I go over. "I'm afraid, Baruch," I whisper.

He gives me a great big bear hug. "I'm here. I won't leave you on your own if you don't want me to, Lidia."

We wait for the nurse to come out of the ER. Then the swinging doors push open, and a nurse in a green uniform appears. Behind her I see a blur of machines and hanging lines of tubes. She sees us, nods, and comes toward us. She's holding a folder in her hand. Her white shoes make no noise.

"It looks like chaos, doesn't it? Don't worry, though. I'll

explain what we're doing in there and then what we want you to do. Is that okay?" She glances at us. Baruch and I nod.

"There are a lot of doctors and nurses in there, a group for each patient. We have to make sure they can breathe, make sure there's blood getting to every part of their bodies, and we've got to keep the heart going. There are ventilators, chest tubes, intravenous lines, x-ray machines. Lots of stuff. It's all there to help." She looks at me again. I nod again. Baruch squeezes my shoulder. My mouth is dry and my hands are shaking. I remember my mother in the hospital, at the end, how awful it was. But this is worse. There is nothing still or white here, it's blood and doctors and nurses talking intensely and urgently. I am scared out of my mind. Please, God, don't let Vera see how afraid I am.

"All of it is to help the surgeon, the orthopedist, the anesthesiologist, and the nurses around each of the beds."

"Of course," Baruch says.

"We don't usually allow visitors into the trauma part of the ER, but there is a very important way you can help."

"How?" I whisper. I can barely get the word out.

The ER door swings open again. I can't help but see shapes lying on the beds, and all the equipment, and it seems as if crowds and crowds of people in green are hunched over like praying mantises. Visitors are not allowed in, she said. I won't have to go in there.

"Netta," someone calls out. She turns around.

"I'm coming," she answers.

I don't want to see what's behind those doors, who is lying on those beds, and how they look. But I can't shut my ears. I hear the moaning and the doctors' orders and the sounds of the equipment. Baruch is holding my hand. His feels warm. He's an old man—isn't he afraid to be in a place like this? A place where people die. How can he be so calm?

The nurse turns back to me. She opens the folder. There are some Polaroid pictures clipped together.

An injured person is rolled past me. Fast, real fast. I see the man's legs but not his face. The nurse and the paramedic wheeling him block my view. There are blood spatters on their green pants. Until the doors swing shut, I hear his breathing. It's like a truck going uphill. The choking, gargling sound he is making frightens me. I feel the room spinning and I want to throw up. I look at the walls. I don't want to see any of this.

All the noise of the hospital machines pumping away, the beep-beep that does not stop. The fluorescent lights make everything look bigger and uglier.

I squeeze Baruch's hand. I want to tell him I feel sick.

The nurse is watching me.

"I know this is hard for you," she says. "I want you to look at these pictures and tell me if there is anything that you recognize."

I don't recognize the person. Whoever it is under the white gauze, whoever it is caught in the tangle of plastic tubes, whoever it is, I don't know them.

"It's not Vera." I turn to Baruch. He also shakes his head.

The nurse moves the photographs downward so the fluorescent lights don't shine directly on them. She puts her arm around my shoulders. "How old are you?"

"I'm nineteen."

"And your name is?"

"Lidia."

"¿Lidia, has estado alguna vez en un hospital?"

Spanish, this nurse knows Spanish! Her words wrap around me like a warm blanket.

Have I ever been in a hospital? My memories of a hospital are bitter and hateful. "Sí. Mi—mi madre," I stutter.

She takes my hand. Mine is sweating, hers is as soft as cream. "Come just a bit closer," she says.

I take a step closer but I can't look at the photographs. I look at the wall instead.

"This is terrible for you, I know. I really do. But you are the only one who can help us. Girls, best friends, they remember things, small things, better than anyone else. So forgive us, forgive me."

She hugs me, this stranger, she understands.

"The patients don't look the same—their faces are covered with gauze, they have suffered terrible injuries, their heads may have been shaved. . . ." She squeezes my hand.

God, they may have cut off all of Vera's hair, her long blond braid she grew when she got to Israel might be gone. In a crazy moment I think: My photograph is wrong, she doesn't look like that anymore, she can't give it to Dan for his birthday.

"Please, Lidia, look at this photograph, just this one, all right? If there's anything that is familiar, some sign, tell me."

I do what she says. I look away from the opposite wall and stare at the photograph she slides out of the folder. It shows hands.

The fingers. The fingers lying on the blanket. The fingers have nail polish on them, pale blue, and each thumb has a little silver star glued on the polish.

"It's Vera," I say, and start to cry. I cry and I can't stop. The nurse puts her arm around me again.

Then she says, "Just one more question, Lidia. Was Vera with someone on the bus?"

I can't think, I just can't think. I shake my head. Vera is in there. Maybe she'll die. I sit down on an empty bench, hide my face, and cry.

Baruch answers instead. "Yes," he says. "She went to the airport to pick up a German volunteer. His name is Thomas Wanninger. He's sixteen, from Berlin. I brought a photograph of him, from his application."

Frau Dürling Aachener Strasse 366, Berlin

"Frau Dürling, you are the most efficient landlady who exists on this earth." All the tenants say that to me. Because in this day and age, efficiency and care have disappeared. Even now, mopping the stairs, I have my system. I swipe the mop from left to right, right to left. I've been doing this for more than thirty years, but I still pay careful attention not to leave streak marks or puddles of water. That's all I need—someone slipping as they hurry down to the front door. Every four or five stairs I squeeze the dirty water out of the mop, move the pail up the few stairs, and start again, left, right, right, left.

I reach the second-floor landing and hear a telephone ringing. I rest the mop on the top stair to listen more carefully. Which apartment is it coming from? Apartment 26. Yes, definitely. The Wanninger apartment. My, my, someone certainly wants to speak to Frau Wanninger.

It is still ringing. I have the key—should I go in? If it rings any longer, I will, I think. I put my hand into my apron pocket. The key ring is there.

The phone continues to ring. Then the ringing stops. Too bad. I had already prepared what to say: "Frau Wanninger is away visiting a cousin in Augsburg. I am Frau Dürling, the landlady. Can I take a message?" Well, no need to go in now.

I wait on the landing. Maybe the person will try again. No, there is no more ringing. Oh well, I will certainly remember to tell Frau Wanninger that her phone rang for a very long while. I squeeze the water out of the mop, move the pail sideways, and begin mopping the landing. She should get an answering machine with Tommi so far away. Maybe I'll tell her. Lots of other things to do today after this. Back and forth, left, right, right, left.

The phone in Frau Wanninger's apartment begins ringing again. I take the keys out of my apron pocket. My hands are wet

94

from the mop and I almost don't manage to turn the doorknob. I hurry in and pick up the receiver on the hall table. A voice asks for Frau Wanninger.

"I am Frau Dürling, the landlady," I explain just as I practiced in my head. "Yes, I have her number. She's at her cousin's in Augsburg. If you can wait, I'll go and get it."

Alex Ushakov Brioni Hotel, Rome

4:35 pm
[ROME TIME]

My lecture is scheduled for 4:45, Critical Advances in Astrophysics Research. I check my papers and my slides—everything is okay, in place. I put all my material into my briefcase and zip it up. I straighten my tie, put on my jacket, and pick up the briefcase. I can hear the television in the next room—WNS and the world business news. Hotel walls are so thin.

I go out and slam the door shut. I put the key card in my pocket. As I pass the adjoining room, I hear, "This is WNS Breaking News." I look at my watch—4:40 pm. I've got five minutes to get to Conference Room #6. I hurry down the hall to the elevator.

The Boss Yoni's Diner, Highway 1

6:10 pm

I saw a soldier running like a madman, zigzagging along the highway. He was shouting "Am I alive? Am I dead? Am I alive?" When the explosion happened, the photograph of Yoni, my son, fell off the wall. I know it means something. It is a sign. Maybe he will be protected but I will pay. My life will end because I am responsible for giving food and water to the evil that made this happen. I lied for Sameh, protected him when the police came around looking for illegal workers, asking if one of them worked for me. And Sameh, who would have believed Sameh could do something like this? I was good to him. Does he hate me? Does he hate all of us? I was a happy man. Now this

95

virus with no cure has ruined all our lives. No one will ever want to come here again. I let him sleep here, eat here, go back to his village. I didn't report him. Nothing. Nothing.

What is there to say? I can't move. My arms are heavy, my head wants to fall forward on my chest, and my legs are like sacks of sand collapsed on the ground. I sit and watch. Seeing but not seeing. Not believing. Not believing.

None of the outside walls are left. The red ambulance lights and the blue lights of the police cars bounce off the exposed nickel walls of the kitchen. The concrete walls of my diner are a pile of nothing. Ben, the cook, is dead. He was outside having a smoke. What will I say to his wife?

The cleanup crew, in their fluorescent vests, move across what used to be my parking lot. They are raking over the ground looking for belongings of those poor people. Behind them, like death's shadows, volunteers carrying black plastic bags search for body parts. Everything that once was a person must be buried. Sanctified. Even the smallest piece of skin or hair, an eyelash, an ankle bone. Nothing is left on the ground. Everything blown off the people on the bus by the power of the explosion is picked up.

I can't hear them, can't hear what they're saying. The noise of the police car sirens and the ambulances is deafening. The men inspect the ground as if there's buried treasure to be found. Like soldier ants they work in rows, up and down, across and back. They move centimeter by centimeter—across the highway, on the sides of the road, in the fields near the road and the parking lot.

The glass of the front window lies in splinters and triangles on top of the rubble of the walls. There is no counter. The cash register is on the floor, the coins and bills are scattered all around. The refrigerator was knocked over on its side. I am sitting at the first table near what once was the revolving door. The clock over the cigarette machine has stopped. On the clock it's

11:47. I sit and watch the graveyard pickers. Yoni's picture is on my lap, the only person I know who is alive, somewhere on an army base, away from this death and destruction, this pile of hate. That's what this is, I say to myself, hate.

I see them stop every few minutes to drink water from bottles. The white plastic gloves they wear make them look like surgeons, but they scoop and swoop like gardeners cleaning a park. I can't stop looking at them. The bags fill up with backpacks, soldiers' duffel bags, a soldier's shirt with sergeant's stripes at the shoulder, pocketbooks, a pink bra, shoes, a baby bottle and a package of disposable diapers, more unlaced shoes. The wind blows a crumpled napkin to the floor. The air smells of smoke, gasoline, burned rubber, and another smell I don't want to think about.

One of the men picks up a strip of cloth, maybe from someone's T-shirt. It could be a piece of Sameh's T-shirt, the one I gave him last month. It had Hebrew lettering. That's how he got on the bus. The bus driver thought he was a Jew. I remember when he first came to me, brought by a Palestinian guy, Omar, who worked in a garage. I didn't think he looked like an Arab.

We all look alike in this damn place.

Five minutes ago the bus was hauled away. The roof was blown off, the inside gutted, the metal body crumpled and twisted, the wheels charred. I heard the bus driver being interviewed on the radio. So far no names of the dead or injured have been announced.

After that the frame and the front bumper of a yellow van were hauled away. The front bumper still had the license plate attached. One of the policemen said the van apparently tried to get into the middle lane, same as the bus. An hour ago the remains of the van's driver were removed in a body bag.

Farmers and workers from the gas station who were here have left behind lit memorial candles. Where did they get them? Is this the land of the dead? Do the living walk around with memorial candles? There are rows and rows of small cans with flickering lights edging the white lines of the parking spaces in the lot. The entrance to my diner looks like a cemetery. Someone has left a bunch of field flowers tied together with string. Mourning has begun, and the names of the dead haven't even been announced. Who knows how many? But there will be dead. Theirs and ours.

6:10 pm **Baruch Ben Tov** Hadarim Hospital

Can you imagine, my Rachel, that I am in charge of a German boy, responsible for his well-being? I am the only one at Kibbutz Broshim who can speak German. His name is Thomas. When he regains consciousness, I will speak *Deutsch*. The language of the soldiers, of the torturers, of the killers. And the words of Goethe and Heine and Schiller, the way my professors spoke them.

He has no father. They are trying to contact his mother. I, a survivor of the ghetto, will escort his mother to his hospital room. After the doctor tells me what to say, I will explain the situation to her in German. Life makes for strange situations, doesn't it, my dear Rachel?

6:10 pm **Clive Burleigh**, WNS Middle East correspondent Zebedeid, Palestinian Authority

We've been granted special permission to come into the village of Zebedeid today. We're here to show you, with our cameras and with interviews, the effect that the death of a suicide bomber has on the place he grew up in.

The sound you're hearing now is the muezzin *calling the faithful of this small village to the prayer,* salahtu el Majrib, *said after the sun sets. Where I'm standing now is the widest road in Zebedeid—no paving, no asphalt, just dust and gravel.*

Walk with me to the village mosque, small and simple in the

sunset light. Only Muslim men can enter the mosque, so let's continue down a side street to see if we can find the women of Zebedeid.

This small house I am standing in front of, unpainted and constructed of cinder blocks, is the house where Sameh Laham grew up. His two brothers have gone to the mosque for the evening prayers. The front door is open.

Sitting on the floor is Sameh's mother with her neighbors and relatives. The women are remembering Abed, Sameh's father. He would have been proud of his son, they say. The crying that you hear, the wails of desolation coming from these women sitting on the floor, the beating of their chests, are an expression of their sadness. But their tears are also tears of pride. Sameh, their Sameh, is now a shaheed. Allah, who is in Heaven, will welcome Sameh. Allah will watch over Sameh's family here on earth. Amal, Sameh's mother, will not be left alone, and her other children will be cared for.

The bareness of this house, the flaking plaster on the walls, expresses the harsh economic realities of this family. The only picture framed and nailed to the bare wall is of the Dome of the Rock mosque in Jerusalem's Old City. Under the picture of the mosque with the golden dome is a verse from the Koran. The verse describes how the Prophet Muhammad rose to Heaven from that very place in Jerusalem. The Palestinian flag is also nailed to the wall: a red triangle and stripes of black, white, and green. Traditionally, each shaheed is covered with the flag as he is carried by a crowd of mourners to his grave.

Nothing in this house resembles an American family home. This is why, as a WNS correspondent, I think it's important for viewers back home to see the level of poverty here. No curtains on the windows, one fluorescent ceiling light, an old refrigerator, a camper's table with a battered television on it. Strangely, there is a brand-new VCR on the floor.

With the help of my interpreter I am going to get more

information from some of the men returning from the evening prayers.

"Two men wearing black jackets with keffiyehs wound around their heads and faces arrived at the village at two in the afternoon. We don't know who they were or where they were from. My cousin took these men to Sameh's house. They had with them a videocassette. It was for Amal, Sameh's mother. One of the men also carried a brand-new video machine. They brought Sameh's last words. Before we went to our prayers we all saw Sameh on the TV."

Sameh Laham's body has not yet been transferred to Zebedeid from the morgue. No one here talks about the damage caused to a body killed in an explosion. It is better to look at the sixteen-year-old alive in a video. I've been told I won't be able to see the video. Apparently here, in Zebedeid, a WNS correspondent is regarded with suspicion as a possible Israeli spy. If you'll bear with me, I can give you a description of it as supplied to me by one of Sameh's friends.

"Sameh is standing in front of the map of our state, the Palestinian state. He holds a Kalashnikov rifle and a Koran. He wears a keffiyeh but his face is not covered, so we know it's him. He stands straight and looks directly at the camera. I can see the scar above his right eye. I remember when he got that scar in a soccer game.

"A voice says: 'Sameh Laham, shaheed for the liberation of Jerusalem, of all of Palestine. Sameh Laham will help return Palestine to all our brothers. The Jews will be gone from our land. Our groves, our orchards, the boundless blue sea, the endless fields will be ours once again.'

"Then our national anthem, 'Baladi, Baladi,' is played. All the time Sameh is looking at the camera.

"Then he speaks: 'I, Sameh Laham, pronounce myself a shaheed. For it is the lives of the martyrs who will make this dream come true.

"'There is nothing greater than being martyred for the sake of Allah, on the land of Palestine. Cry only in joy, my mother. Hand out dates, my brothers, for your son and brother awaits a wedding in Heaven.

"'Consider those who have died for the sake of Allah not as dead, but rather as alive, who are being nurtured by their Lord.

"'And say not of those who are slain in the way of Allah: "They are dead." Nay, they are living, though ye perceive it not.'

"We all danced and sang; we did as Sameh would have wished. We were happy for him. Dates were passed around. But we did not put sugar in the coffee we drank. We drank sahda because we are in mourning.

"His mother was crying, but also smiling."

Did she say anything? I asked.

"Yes," Sameh's friend answered. "She said she was sad to lose Sameh but she knew he was alive in God's company. She was proud, very, very proud.

"We will see the video many, many times. People will come from other villages to see it."

Behind me, the sanctification of Sameh Laham has begun. Two boys, classmates of Sameh, undeterred by the evening darkness, using flashlights, are beginning to paint his likeness on all the available walls of this village. Tomorrow the face of the sixteen-year-old suicide bomber will stare back at the villagers from the walls of the school, the grocery, the garage, and the repair shop here in Zebedeid.

This is Clive Burleigh for WNS.

11:00 PM Radio newscast

This is the eleven o'clock evening news. At 11:47 this morning a suicide bomber exploded himself on the number 9 bus traveling to Jerusalem. We are now able to report the names of the dead:

> *Private Samuel Horoshovsky, age 19, Haifa*
> *Private Anna Gilad, age 18, Haifa*
> *First Lieutenant Rashid el-Azayzeh, age 21, Sahur*
> *Leila Al-Kahlout, age 26, en-El-Qadi*
> *Mervat Al-Kahlout, age 4 months, en-El-Qadi*
> *Arin Al-Kahlout, age 22, en-El-Qadi*
> *Anat Mamilyan, age 16, Kiryat Gat*
> *Sara Levy, age 63, Kiryat Gat*
> *Yael Levy, age 45, Kiryat Gat*
> *Benny Davidov, age 13, Beersheba*
> *Haim Davidov, age 52, Beersheba*
> *Sergeant Yuval Bar, age 23, Tel Aviv*
> *Sergeant Ron Kovarski, age 23, Jerusalem*
> *Sally Cochran, age 32, Boston*
> *Tom Linker, age 29, Boston*
> *Brad Holerbie, age 27, Minneapolis*
> *Yasir Rajoub, age 41, Nazareth*
> *Jaber Rajoub, age 6, Nazareth*
> *Ben Zelkovitz, age 38, Mevasseret*

May they rest in peace.
The suicide bomber has been identified as Sameh Laham, 16, of Zebedeid. So far no terrorist group has claimed responsibility.

For inquiries about the injured, a twenty-four-hour hotline is open at Hadarim Hospital.

MONDAY, APRIL 10

I sit down on the edge of Vera's bed. I'm still in my uniform. I still don't believe she's not here waiting for me. What is it that people say? One event, one phone call, can change your life.

It was past midnight when the vegetable truck I'd hitched a ride on left me off at the main gate of the kibbutz. Past the watchman's booth there were blue lights flashing from the roof of a police car. In the distance, I saw, the community hall was all lit up inside. Something horrible, worse than I'd been told, had happened. What?

The watchman in the booth confirmed what I'd heard on the phone—just a simple sentence: Yes, your girlfriend's been injured and so has the volunteer she went to pick up. When I got to my house, I told my parents I wanted to go to the hospital right away. They told me that Baruch had just come back from there.

I crossed the field to Baruch's house. He told me she was in serious but stable condition. He would go back again in while, and I would go with him.

The bedsprings creak and somewhere outside a crow is cawing. There are no other sounds at this hour.

Only the screen covers the window. I smell the sharpness of the wet grass outside. The warm night air stirs and fingers the things here in her room. I unlace and yank off my dusty black army boots. I put the pillow under my head. It smells of her. I stretch out. The cotton blanket is lumpy and soft under my legs. I keep looking at the snapshots she has taped to the wall: us at the beach, us hiking, and us just lounging on the couch in my house. On the night table her dried flowers and the university application. Still blank. She promised it would be filled in by the end of the week. No, I can't be angry at her now. How can I? I just want her to live.

How can she die? She's so alive. The snapshots almost move with her breath, or is it my heart pounding?

We made up our own language, stupid words but to us our private code. Who will I talk to now? Suddenly I'm dead tired. Wiped out. My hands are shaking. I've never thought much about God. Not my thing to ask for help or look up at the sky and talk to some kind of power up there. But now my lips are moving. Words I've never said before: God, please, please, let her live. A breeze lifts up the leaves of the small ivy plant. Is it an answer?

I get up and go to the window. In the moonlight the lawns are dark purple and the flowers dots of white and silver. Of course touching her excites me. There's something more, though. She's my friend, my best friend. I look around the room. Her hair-brush, some colored rubber bands for her braid, botany books, a photo of her in her ballet class when she was ten. There are days and years of her life I wasn't a part of. Sometimes she cries, very suddenly, for no reason. I ask her to tell me why, but she shakes her head. I want to know everything because I am giving her *my* life. I don't want her to be afraid. I'm not. And no matter what she ever tells me or does, I'll never stop loving her. We've been waiting for each other all our lives.

I hear slow footsteps coming up the stairs. Baruch opens the door. "It's time to go, isn't it?" He nods. I pull my boots on.

Clive Burleigh, WNS Middle East correspondent Road to
Hadarim Hospital

4:20 AM

"Will we go past where the bus explosion was?" I ask.

The tall, dark, bearded man who's my driver shakes his head.
"It happened on Highway 1, which is down there. We're in the
Judean Hills now, above the highway, on the road to the hospi-
tal. When there's more light, you'll be able to see the location."

There's a local cameraman sitting in the front of the van. He
and the driver talk, short terse sentences in Hebrew. I'm left out.
Doesn't bother me, I'm here to draw my own conclusions.

"I am so sorry," I said to the driver when he picked me up at
Ben Gurion Airport.

"Thanks. Being on the bus, or in the restaurant, it's fate," he
answered. "Fate." I must have heard that word a hundred times
since I came—*goral* in Hebrew.

"It's fate," the cameraman says to me as if he's reading my
mind, "the explosion happening at a place so close to the hospital. We were lucky."

He uses the word "we" as if he's personally involved. I'll
remember that. Maybe I'll lead off with it. I don't think anything
about this incident is lucky, but I don't comment. The driver
checks the rearview mirror and accelerates.

"Any final figures on the injured and dead?" I ask.

"No," the driver answers.

No one speaks for a long time. Then the driver makes a sharp
right turn. "This is the same road the ambulances took," he
says.

"Amazing how fast they got there," I say.

"Yes, minutes. The hospital began receiving victims in less
than twenty minutes."

The cameraman whispers something to the driver. He nods
and turns the radio on. "I'll translate for you if there's anything
important," the cameraman says.

107

I see the outlines of trees and hilly slopes, but that is all. Didn't King David write a psalm about these hills outside Jerusalem, the Judean Hills? From somewhere I remember that. But for all I can see, I might just as well be in the countryside outside my house back home. I stare at the asphalt road. How will I report this—is it the story of one person, or a family, or the driver? Will victims want to talk to me? Will anyone be conscious?

The car ashtray is full of stale cigarette butts, but the driver isn't smoking. I can see the bulge of a cigarette pack in his shirt pocket. I want a cigarette—smoking is an old working trick of mine. I refocus on the road, on whatever I can see of the scenery.

The road is narrow, and the driver navigates the curves and steep inclines slowly and carefully. None of us talks. The radio reports fill the sound gap. So far no one is translating for me.

"Anything new?" I ask. They shake their heads. That is the last attempt at polite conversation. We go back to silence.

The traffic is heavy, a line of headlights piercing the dark in front of us and behind us. Cars traveling to the hospital, the cameraman explains. There can be no other destination at this hour of the night on this road. The lights disappear in the bends and then reappear again as the road straightens.

I look at my watch. Almost dawn and Monday. For other people, someplace else, the beginning of an ordinary Monday, but for those of us in the van it will be a long and endless story about death and tragedy. One day I suppose I'll explain to my kids that my job is reporting and recording people's hatred of one another.

The driver suddenly hits the brakes. Behind us a screeching sound of tires as the car following us comes to a halt. A deer skitters across the black asphalt into the forest. Inside the van there is a sound of relief at not having to see death, not a deer, not a rabbit, not any creature. The driver steps on the gas. We pick up speed again.

We pull into a large stone-paved plaza. It is packed with people and cars. The driver mutters something under his breath. I'm checking my shoulder bag for pocket recorder, identification, press tag. The cameraman is checking his equipment. The driver rolls down the window and puts his head out, searching in all directions for a parking space. The sky is still night black, but the white projector lights beaming from the building turn the square into daylight. We can't move forward or backward, we're stuck in a line of taxis and cars. Ambulances and police cars encircle the ER entrance. Until they pull out, nothing else can move. The driver beeps the horn at the taxi in front of him.

I understand nothing of the Hebrew, not the signs or what people are saying. Only the English letters above the entrance have any meaning: EMERGENCY ROOM. But I've been here before, I say to myself. The same stretchers were being carried in Bosnia, in Rwanda, in Northern Ireland. Can I use the material I read from in those places? Maybe. But of course I reject the idea, because although there may be a sameness to war, each human being is a world unto himself. My job is to report what I see, what I discover, but it is always to respect these people, their history, their tragedies, their hopes.

The van inches forward slowly. It's warm. Well, it's April in Israel, almost summer.

As we move closer to the entrance, I see, from the van window, the numb faces, the people clutching at each other, children and adults hugging and moaning. "Many are in shock," the driver says. "They have no visible injuries, but they will keep coming for hours, even days, after an attack."

"The walking wounded," I comment.

"Yes," he agrees.

The cameraman switches off the car radio.

In here I don't hear the wailing of the ambulances. We push our way through the crowd milling just beyond the doors in the corridor. At the information desk, I explain who we are, why we're here.

The entrance area inside the hospital is jammed with what looks like hundreds of people. Is everyone related to someone on the bus? That's impossible. There must be friends here and neighbors. There is no calm hospital silence. People cry, cell phones ring, every nurse and doctor is stopped and asked for information. The two of us are almost swallowed up. I try not to think about what is happening in the corridors off this space. I concentrate on pushing with Baruch through the crowds. The fluorescent ceiling fixtures above my head light up everything and everybody, clearly and painfully. Mixed in with the weeping families are newspaper reporters and a television crew. Someone with a WNS press tag. And men in Arab headdress. We all live here, don't we?

A nurse tells someone that she is going to the orthopedic ward, and I hurry down the hallway after her. Religious Jewish women in long dresses and turbans covering their heads move aside for us, high school kids with soda cans in their hands, volunteers passing out paper cups of coffee. Ten men stand in a corner praying. Pray for Vera, I want to say. A woman holding a transistor radio listens to the news while her little boy plays on the floor. I nearly trip over him. If this explosion hadn't happened, he would be fast asleep in his bed.

5:02 AM **Baruch Ben Tov** Intensive care unit—Neurology, Hadarim Hospital

At the desk outside the ICU, the nurse explains what's happening to Thomas Wanninger. The staff has been given the information I supplied. They know he doesn't speak Hebrew, that he was on his way to Broshim as a volunteer.

I follow the nurse into the room. In the middle of the large space is a circular nurses' station with a view of the six cubicles. Two of the cubicles are enclosed by curtains. People are sitting near some of the beds. They look up for a minute, notice me, stare, and turn away. Mothers, fathers? Wives, husbands?

I ask the nurse if he has started to speak. "That's what I'm here for," I tell her. "I can speak to him in German."

"He's in a coma. He doesn't hear or react to anything at the moment. But it's good that you're here. He needs the stimulation of hearing someone speak, and of course if it's German, his own language . . . The more you talk to him, the better his chances of recovery, of coming out of the coma."

There is almost no sound in this room, only the whirring and beeping of machines and the words of encouragement whispered to the patients.

The nurse points to the bed opposite the door. "I'll bring you a chair," she says.

"Thank you."

When I sit down I tell her, "I will stay. He is alone, you know."

"Of course," says the nurse. "If you decide to stay through the night, we'll find someplace for you to rest. We need your help. Certainly until a relative arrives."

"Yes, I don't know when the mother will arrive. From Berlin." I pronounce *Berlin* the way a German would. The nurse notices.

"What a blessing for this boy that you speak German and that you are here," she says.

Odd to consider that I am a blessing for this boy.

The nurse pulls the curtain around the bed and leaves us alone. Now I really look at him. His face is red from the burns, his eyebrows and hair singed. There is a thick bandage across his forehead. His body is very still. Not the nice-looking young man in the photograph.

Talk to him. The nurse says that will help him. But what? All I can think of is flowers. Well, why not?

Bei uns im Kibbutz lessen wir wunderbare Blumen wachsen, fast jede art—nelken Rosen, Narzissen, Gladiolen, Margariten. . . .

5:02 AM **Dan Oron** Orthopedic ward—room 414, Hadarim Hospital

I follow the nurse down the hall.

"She's in here. She's sedated but you can sit next to her."

There are two other beds in the room but they're empty. Vera's is the last one, near the window.

When I see her, I start to cry.

"It's okay, it's okay." The nurse gives me a hug, like I'm a baby. A guy in an army uniform.

"She's in severe pain. We've listed her condition as moderate to severe. The good news is she's stable. She'll be receiving fluids to replace what she's losing through the wounds, and lots of care. It will all take time."

"What about her eye? With the patch? Will she see?"

"Yes. Look, just sit next to her. You can talk to her if you want to. Even though she can't hear you, it may help her, and probably it'll help *you*. Okay?"

I nod. "I heard they pulled her out from under a seat in the bus."

The nurse shakes her head. "I didn't see her in ER or the operating room, so I don't know the details. But . . ."

"Yes?" What else did she want to tell me?

"Look, she's probably going to have the hardest time when she begins to remember what she saw. So her friends and family are going to have to be patient."

"Her parents aren't here, they're in Odessa."

"Well, she's got you and that lovely girl, her best friend, right? And people from the kibbutz. I'm sure she'll get lots of support. If you need me, I'm just up the hall."

"Before you go, can you tell me about all this stuff she's hooked up to?"

"Don't be concerned about it. As she gets better, we'll start to remove the assistance."

"Like the oxygen mask?"

"Yes."

She leaves.

I see the cuts, the bruises, the bandages on her neck, her arm, her leg, the patch on her eye. Parts of her hair were singed, and her naked scalp shows. The blond hair that is left has turned soot black. I kiss her forehead. Gently, no more pain, Vera. I'm here.

Lidia comes in. From where? "She looks awful, doesn't she?" Tears begin to stream down her face. "Baruch says she's young and strong."

"He's right. We should just be glad she's alive," I say. "Did you see the picture of the bus?"

"Yes. I can't believe they got her out of there."

"Well, they did. How's the boy? The volunteer?"

"He's in a coma. Baruch is with him now. It's good that he went back to rest. For an old man like him, this must be even worse."

There are dark circles under her eyes. "Look, Lidia, you've got to get out of here. Take a break," I tell her. "I think you should go back to the kibbutz. I'll stay here."

Finally Lidia agrees. When I'm alone, I bend over and kiss Vera again. "I'm here, I love you. I love you."

I've been home an hour. I keep looking at the clock, I don't know why. An hour ago, at five, Ruthie brought me back from the hospital. How long was I there? Forever, I think. You're in shock, the nurse said, but first we have to treat the seriously wounded. If she knew who I was, she would have spit on me. One of the nurses gave me some water and told me to sit down and wait. Please, God, I said, don't let them ask me who I am, the owner, Sameh's boss.

Finally the nurse took my blood pressure and checked my heart. My body was shaking like an earthquake was inside of it. I couldn't stop trembling even when I squeezed my arms over my chest and crossed my legs. The emergency room nurse gave me a bottle of pills. Come back in two or three days, she said to me in a very quiet voice, if you don't feel better. Everyone has this reaction, she said to reassure me. I almost told her, "But not everyone has a dishwasher who is a suicide bomber."

Every bone in my body was still shaking when we got home. Ruthie said, Lie down and rest. I can't. I walk around the apartment like an animal in a cage. I hear Ruthie crying. I tell her to leave me alone.

I'll never be able to look at the people I know from the restaurant. If the parents of the kids who were killed on the bus want to come and kill me, I'll let them. I understand. I'm to blame. Sameh worked for me.

About an hour ago light started to come through the closed shutters. Let me open the windows, Ruthie said. No, I don't want anyone to see me, to know I'm here. I wouldn't let her turn on the six o'clock morning news. I don't want to hear the names of the dead.

Yoni is on his way home. It's his last week of army service. I was going to close the restaurant next Thursday night and turn the place into a party for him and all his buddies. Now what will I do? What will he say to me?

Ruthie, I say, let me tell you what happened. My whole body shakes and I tell her, and I keep telling her. How I ran into the kitchen when I heard the explosion. Ben wasn't there. All the time running outside to grab a cigarette. Then I saw that Sameh wasn't there and I knew in my guts he had something to do with it. Ruthie, listen, there was a high school girl who wanted more ketchup on her hamburger and then she was under the counter screaming, "They're killing me, Mommy, come, I'm going to die."

I can't go back there, I tell Ruthie. How will we live? How will I take care of my family? Yoni will say I killed the soldiers on the bus as surely as if I'd taken a gun and shot them. All because I trusted Sameh. He's better off than I am. At least he's dead.

Are all the shutters closed, Ruthie? I want the house to be dark, like my life now. I'm shaking, the water is spilling out of the glass, the floor is wet. Ruthie, come and help me take my pills. Now go away, Ruthie.

Maybe I'll take the whole bottle of pills.

Security Service headquarters, somewhere in Jerusalem   6:10 AM

SENIOR AGENT: Have you traced the yellow van?
AGENT: Yes, the owner was in last night.
SENIOR AGENT: And . . . ?
AGENT: And the bad news is we guessed wrong. The only chance of getting substantial information is if this kid, Sameh, talks.
SENIOR AGENT: I want guards around the clock. Day and night. Don't leave him alone. He'll break, and I want someone there when he does. Have someone in there who knows the Arabic slang he talks. Chat him up, but no religious stuff. Talk about home, remind him of his mother, his brothers and sisters. He's

soft. They know they made a mistake with him. Either they'll try to get to him or he'll do something to himself.

AGENT: Understood.

SENIOR AGENT: What a mistake we made, what a mistake! We have to find out who sent Omar.

AGENT: What are we going to do about Sameh's boss?

SENIOR AGENT: The boss? The owner of the place, you mean? Yes, of course. You're right. He'll have to be charged.

AGENT: What about Omar's family?

SENIOR AGENT: They're probably as surprised as we are.

6:30 AM **Clive Burleigh**, WNS Middle East correspondent Joulani family home, Jabel Fahm, Palestinian Authority

The picture Ahmed Joulani is holding is a picture of his son, Omar.

"Allahu akbar"—Allah is great—is what is being shouted by the villagers and relatives of Omar Joulani. The men in this village have refused to speak to the WNS crew; even our interpreter, a Palestinian, has not been able to find someone willing to comment on Omar's death, or to name the organization that sent him on his suicide mission. Jabel Fahm is a terrorist stronghold—many of the suicide bombers have come from here or nearby villages.

Those are gunshots you hear. It is customary to fire guns in the air as a sign of emotion, or identification with the bereaved.

"Ya shaheed, beloved of God, rest, rest, ya shaheed."

"Omar," wails his father, "a month ago you said you wanted to be a shaheed."

The voice you're hearing, together with mine, is that of our crew interpreter.

The father keeps kissing Omar's photograph.

"Yaba, yaba, may Allah have mercy on him," he is shouting. As you can see, the circle of men is unable to calm him down.

"Leave me alone," he says. "Let me cry, let me cry. Let Allah hear me. Let Allah bring my son back to me, back to his village."

A man is shouting to everyone in the room. "The blood of every shaheed is soaking the land of Palestine, it is mixing with the sweet dew. We will struggle until every Israeli is dead and the Jews are driven from the land."

"Yes, we swear in the names of the fallen that our oath is unbreakable. The end is near and it will be glorious."

Rashida, Omar's mother, sits with the women in a separate circle. She chants her story again and again.

"I baked my pitot early in the morning, to give my son his breakfast. At one o'clock in the afternoon someone called me and said a yellow van from the garage where Omar worked had blown up.

"'My son, my son,' I screamed to the person, 'where is my son?' I didn't know what to do with myself, where to go, who to ask about Omar. How could I go to the police, who could I ask if he was wounded, maybe dying? Who? Who? Tell me. I wrapped the pitot in a clean cloth so they would be ready for him when he came back. How foolish I was." She has started to cry again. Her body is doubled over in grief and she covers her face with the long white scarf she wears wound around her head.

"My life is destroyed, I have no life now. He gave us his earnings, everything, so we could live. Oh, Allah, has there ever been a son like that?"

This is Clive Burleigh, with the WNS crew, reporting from Jabel Fahm.

Amal Laham Zebedeid, Palestinian Authority   *6:30 AM*

I do not think the Israeli soldiers will come here this week. Omar Joulani from Jabel Fahm is dead. My Sameh is alive. Allah, I cannot believe it, alive! I am afraid to go outside. Someone in the village has painted the word *khayen* on the door. To swear on the Koran that you will be a *shaheed* and to escape death by an act of cowardice, that is to be a traitor. I am the mother of a traitor—*khayen*—but in my heart I am happy.

The children are still sleeping. When they wake up, I will tell them about Sameh. Today I will keep them inside. I will cover the window with our flag, with the Palestinian flag. Then maybe the one who wrote *khayen* on my wall will leave us alone.

7:15 AM **Vera Brodsky** Orthopedic ward—room 414, Hadarim Hospital

"Papa, look at my spins." Papa is sitting on a bench at the ice-skating rink. He's reading. I want him to put his book down and look at me.

Now he's waving. "I'm watching, Verushka." Then he shouts, "Bravo, you look like a champion!"

7:15 AM **Dan Oron** Orthopedic ward—room 414, Hadarim Hospital

Vera has opened her eyes once or twice but immediately closed them. The beep of the monitor does not change, nor the pale green curves on the screen.

Downstairs I met one of the medics from the ambulance. "I told her talk, talk, don't worry what you say, just talk, stay with us," he said.

All I could say to him was "Thanks." Stupid, I guess, but what can you say to a guy who saved Vera and then gets into an ambulance and does it again for someone else?

I've looked at the chart. Her left arm and leg have been operated on. There's a problem with her left eye. I don't understand the medical terms.

I get up and go out of the room to find the nurse. The nurse says, "Be patient, Dan, it will take time until she can speak." So I sit next to the bed and stare at all the tubes and machinery keeping her alive.

"Next year we're going to university together," I tell the nurse. "She's a phenomenal botanist, you know, the kind of person who can make plants grow in the desert. She doesn't even know how good she is. She still can't make up her mind about us, about her studies."

I'm running on and on like someone's wound me up. The nurse goes out and brings me a cup of water and a small white pill.

"I'm sorry, I can't stop talking."

"It's okay. It's normal. You're just having a reaction to all of this."

"I won't leave her. You know, she said things were going so well, too well. So something terrible was bound to happen. How did she know?"

"She didn't know. Really. No one can know about something as terrible as this. It's just a feeling people get sometimes." She put the pill into my hand. "Here, swallow this. It will help."

"I won't leave her." I swallow the pill and drink some water.

A different nurse comes in and puts a folding cot in the corner of the room. I call my commanding officer. He gives me as much leave as I need. Then I call my parents and ask them to bring me clean clothes. Another patient has been brought into the room. I draw the curtains around Vera's bed and sit close to the bed. I'm beginning to feel sleepy.

Baruch Ben Tov Intensive care unit—Neurology, Hadarim Hospital   7:15 AM

In this intensive care unit there are no windows. The lights are on twenty-four hours a day—there is no day, no night. In Vera's ward there are fake windows. The artificial light behind them changes with the hours. The nurse explained that they've discovered that people like to know if it is day or night. It comforts them to have that knowledge. But here there are just walls.

I've been up to the fourth floor to see Vera. Dan is with her. "We're guarding the gates," I said to Dan.

"Let no evil spirit enter these rooms." He laughed. The young don't know about evil.

In a little while, I'll get some breakfast and then go visit Vera again.

The coma is disturbing. The doctors tell me it is caused by a swelling of the brain. They hope that in a few days Thomas will start to come out of it.

This morning I am a little more used to his stillness. I no longer expect the boy lying in the bed to be the boy who sent us his photo. Only a strong pinch or pinprick from the doctor or nurse draws a reaction, and then it is not a yell or a shout, it is a deep throaty sound and a body spasm.

Outside in the waiting room the bright sun shines through the window blinds. When I look down at the entrance, I see the palm trees bend with the spring wind. A beautiful day. Maybe I will sleep here tonight. After all, I am responsible for him.

I called Berlin yesterday and spoke to a Herr Speyer at Hanseatic Insurance. I also spoke to a Frau Dürling, the landlady of the apartment house. Strange to hear the German words coming out of my mouth, so automatically, so naturally. What one learns when one is young is never forgotten.

Frau Dürling told me she was feeding the bird and watering the plants in the Wanninger apartment. Thomas's story has been in all the newspapers and on television. The German embassy in Israel has also provided information. Contact with his mother is a matter of a few more hours.

The hospital social worker informed me that none of the boy's personal possessions have been found.

Early this morning a twelve-year-old girl died from the shrapnel in her head. The doctors could not operate on her. Her parents donated her organs. She will live on.

This morning, while the doctors did their examinations, Dan

and I went down to the hospital cafeteria. When we sat down, he said to me, "You know, the first thing I'll say to Thomas's mother is that I don't blame Thomas for what happened to Vera. She loved going to the airport to meet the volunteers. No one was better at it than she was. She could make someone feel at home in a minute."

He poured more milk into his coffee and looked around at the people in the cafeteria. I sipped my tea. We took the elevator up to the third and fourth floors. We didn't say anything—there didn't seem to be anything left to say.

Sameh Laham, security prisoner 0593 Surgical ward— Isolation, Hadarim Hospital   7:15 AM

The doctors have put a needle in my arm, it is connected to a plastic bag with liquid. When I ask the nurse, she says it gives my body back the liquids it has lost. The next time I wake up, I ask again. It is another nurse and she says the same thing. But I think it is poison. What will happen to me if I take the needle out? Will the poison stop coming into my body? But I'll die anyway. I'm a suicide bomber. I close my eyes. The pain is terrible. I am here but very far away. My body has moved away from my head. I am two people.

I'm never alone in this room. Two policemen are here all the time. When they talk to each other, they say it is a miracle I am alive. They know I understand Hebrew. They talk about me as if I'm dead. Living dead, that's what I am. I've made up my mind not to say anything. If it's a slow poison, how long do I have to live?

It is daylight. I can see the sun. My head feels like a sack of sand. I can't move my fingers, they feel cold. The room is turning around me and the ceiling moves up and down. I will never be able to escape. A nurse has explained in Arabic that my liver was damaged. That is why, she said, you feel so weak. But you will recover.

121

I wonder all the time how many people in the bus died. Did the mother and her baby die? Allah knows. I slipped the backpack off. I did nothing. I let it fall. If only I hadn't seen her on the bus.

One policeman is sitting by the door drinking coffee. He looks up. I quickly close my eyes. I hear him get up. He is near my bed. Maybe he has orders to kill me, here in the hospital, where no one will know. I open my eyes and stare at him.

"Just checking the IV bag," he says. He talks Arabic to me. "After all, we want to keep you alive."

My head is drumming. Does my mother know I'm alive? Now there will be no money for her. I will have to go back to work for the Boss. No, of course not, am I so stupid? I'll be in jail. Everything, my whole life, is very far away. I want to vomit. Is this part of dying?

2:00 PM **Baruch Ben Tov** Hadarim Hospital

Ilse Wanninger has arrived in Israel. I spent the morning with her at the hospital. When she came, the doctors were examining Thomas. She sat in the waiting room. I explained everything to her. She listened intently and smiled gratefully. I am somewhat embarrassed by how thankful she is for my presence, for the fact that I speak her language. I cannot be angry with her for making me speak German.

She seems to be a kind woman. She must have been pretty when she was younger. She has large brown eyes and short graying black hair. I thought when I first met her that she could have been Jewish. She is not tall. Thomas must have inherited his height from his father.

She explains that now that her husband is dead, her whole life revolves around Thomas. "I wanted to have many children. Both Otto and I are children of parents who fought in—" She stops suddenly and looks away.

"Are you afraid to mention the war?"

She stares at her hands. "It is very difficult for me, Herr Ben Tov."

"Frau Wanninger, what has happened is terrible. Luckily Thomas is alive. We will help you and Thomas to get through this." She clasps and unclasps her hands. She stares away from them, out, toward me. She sees the number on my arm. She draws in her breath. It is almost a gasp.

I do not move. I do not say anything. I continue to sit opposite her. I expected this moment, but I expected it with the boy. I do not explain anything. I say nothing about myself, nothing about *the* war, *any* war. I am too old and, just now, too tired. I do not have the strength. She will have to learn that every man on the face of the earth is wounded and only doctors have the right to remove bandages.

"What I want to say to you is, I know how you have suffered in this country. You have had many wars here, and Jews have been in many wars. . . ."

I nod.

"You do not mind if I explain something to you about us, about Thomas?"

What can I say? "No, of course not." People in the waiting room look at us, two people talking in a foreign language.

"Thomas is my only child. . . ." She stops, as if she is looking for the right words.

I must cut off these confidences. We all have a story, don't we? "Frau Wanninger, you are a courageous woman to have let Thomas come to Israel. Not many mothers would let their child come here. After all, we're not the quietest spot in the world. It is brave to permit your sixteen-year-old son to come here, even for a short time."

"I have something to tell you, Herr Ben Tov."

She is determined to tell me her story. I am trapped. I see that the philodendron plant on the corner table needs water.

"I have to tell you why Thomas *really* came here." She looks up. A nurse comes into the waiting room. "Yes?" she asks.

"The doctors are still examining Tommi, Mrs. Wanninger. It will be a while."

Her face falls.

"There is nothing you have to tell us," I say firmly. "Really. We were happy to accept him. Every volunteer is welcome at the kibbutz. At their age they are enthusiastic—they want to get away from home for a bit. . . ."

"Yes, you're right. That is what he told his school principal. But there is another reason, the real reason."

"Surely, Frau Wanninger, there are things Tommi would like you to keep as a secret. Between you and him." I do not know what she wants to tell me. There is suddenly an insane desire on my part to be out of here, back with my plants, my music, peace and quiet without people.

"He came here to fulfill a wish of his father's."

That startles me. What wish would bring the son of a German veterinarian to Israel?

She stands up. She walks over to the window and stares out. The sun lights her face. She looks very tired.

I want to bring this talk to an end. I feel the sticky dampness of sweat under my armpits, and my pulse is racing. I have no medication with me.

"Frau Wanninger, shall I speak with the doctors? Maybe they will tell me something more." I say it softly and in slow, precise German, so that it will calm her and give me a chance to leave her and go down the corridor to the nurses' station. I must take a pill as soon as possible or I will collapse.

"Yes, you are right." She seems relieved that I stopped the conversation. "After all, they want to give a mother hope. But they will be more honest with you, Herr Ben Tov."

I get up and walk down the hall. I tell one of the nurses that my heart is pounding and I am prone to anxiety attacks and high blood pressure. "I do not want the boy's mother to know I am not feeling well," I explain.

Out of sight of Ilse Wanninger, she leads me into an examining room. She takes my blood pressure and then gives me a tranquilizer. I lie down on the examining table. When I feel better, I ask about Tommi's condition. The nurse reassures me that Dr. Stitti and the ICU nurses are certain Tommi will come out of the coma. The only question is when.

After a few minutes I feel calmer. I return to Ilse Wanninger. "The nurses say they are hopeful Tommi will be all right, he will come out of the coma. They have told me exactly what they've told you."

"Hopeful but not sure?"

"No, 'certain' is what they said. Really."

We go into the room. Tommi is lying very still, his eyes closed. His fingers are black, bent, and bruised. It will be a long time before he plants anything in a garden.

Do you know, young man, I prepared your work schedule and I went to your room. I left it for you, never thinking you wouldn't arrive. We missed meeting each other by a few hours and the act of a crazy man.

Baruch Ben Tov Returning to Kibbutz Broshim   2:30 PM

I say goodbye to Ilse Wanninger and leave the hospital. I do not board the bus for the kibbutz. I take a different bus to where the ancient walls encircle the city of Jerusalem. I wander the narrow streets. Jerusalem. Eternal Jerusalem. I find myself outside a church. I go in. The front rows are filled with people. I sit down in a pew in the back. The afternoon light forms uneven pools of gold on the stone floor. An organ begins to play. It is Bach. A deep bass voice sings.

"Endlich, endlich wird mein Joch
wieder von mir weichen müessen . . ."

I cover my face with my hands. Rachel, my own, Rachel, Ruchele, tell me what to do now. Only you know what I did.

" . . . Oh! gescheh es heute noch."

Finally, finally will my yoke again have to be lifted from me. . . . Oh, may it happen today.

I leave the church and walk until I finally reach a bus stop. I sit on the bench and wait for the bus that will take me back to the kibbutz.

The bus drives through the winding cobbled streets and then leaves the city. It cuts through the heart of the Judean Hills. I am standing in afternoon shadow when I open the door of my house.

2:30 PM **Vera Brodsky** Orthopedic ward—room 414, Hadarim Hospital

I am moving down a corridor. Sharp fluorescent lights color everything white-blue, it's all gigantic in size. I'm in a shopping mall with Sergei. We've come to buy suitcases. I am walking but Sergei is in a wheelchair. Papa has promised to meet us here. There he is. He is standing with Katerina. She's pregnant. Her stomach is very big, and she is wearing Mama's blue checkered dress. Katerina is looking at a toy store window full of stuffed animals. Oh, Alex, she says, and points to a pink penguin. It's so sweet, she says. The baby will love it. She goes with Papa into the store. I keep moving, pushing Sergei's wheelchair toward the toy store so I can meet Papa. The marble floor of the mall is slick, there are no bumps or sudden turns or curves. It is easy for me to push the wheelchair. Almost like sliding it over ice. I used to ice-skate.

Look, Sergei, there's my father. He's in the toy store. He doesn't see us. I don't want to be here, Sergei says in a tired voice. Let's leave this place, Verushka. But I don't listen to him. I keep moving to the toy store. There's the luggage store, I say. I'll just get Papa, and he'll buy us the suitcases. No, Verushka, he says. I don't need a suitcase anymore. Oh, you're joking again, Sergei. Enough, Verushka, I want to go home.

I keep pushing the wheelchair. Then I smell smoke. There are flames coming out of the toy store. What should I do? Leave Sergei alone and run to Papa? The flames are spreading through the mall. The flames are in the bus. Please, Sergei, tell me what to do. But Sergei has disappeared. I'm alone. I am under a seat in a bus. I run toward the store but I keep falling. Something is wrong with my legs. I scream out, Papa, I'm coming, I'm coming. Something is holding me down. . . . I am being lifted.

I wake up. Papa. Mama. They are *here.* Papa standing, Mama next to him. Together. How strange. Papa bends over, he kisses me, Mama is crying, her hands are near my head, she wants to smooth my hair.

"You're out of intensive care, Verushka. You're going to be fine," Papa whispers. I feel his breath on my eyelashes.

A grating buzzing goes around and around in my ears, like a hundred bees. I want to explain it to Papa, who's a scientist, but my body is far away from my voice and I am flying away, so fast I don't have time to say I'll be back, wait for me here, please. Then I see the German boy's face, Tommi's face. Where is Tommi? Babushka, if Mama is here, then you are all alone. Irena can't help you if you don't feel well. Everybody has been deserted. Mama, Papa, I want to tell you all about Dan, I want to tell you how happy I am. So much to tell. I hurt so much.

———— SURPRISE ARREST ————

JERUSALEM, ISRAEL, MONDAY, APRIL 10. Israeli police have admitted holding a Palestinian teenager as a suspect in the number 9 bus explosion. The suspect has been identified as Sameh Laham, 16, from the village of Zebedeid. Though the police refuse to comment on the boy's physical condition or his precise whereabouts, unnamed sources acknowledge that he is at Hadarim Hospital, under heavy police guard.

Preliminary investigation has shown that the bus was not blown up from the inside. A vehicle drove alongside the bus and then detonated the powerful bomb. The extremist group Islamic Jihad has claimed responsibility for the act. They have identified the driver of the vehicle, a stolen van, as Omar Joulani, 18, from the village of Jabel Fahm.

A reliable police source commented: "Be assured that the prisoner, injured or not, will face intensive interrogation. We will uncover all links between Laham and Joulani and the people who provided the explosives. If there are other terrorist groups involved, we will also uncover that."

A physician at Hadarim Hospital, who wished to remain anonymous, said: "On the same floor of the hospital we are treating one of the suicide bombers and eleven people injured in the attack. Twelve human beings are suffering together within the space of a few meters. I cannot think of another place in the world where this could happen."

Does the doctor think close contact of this nature will change relations between the Palestinians and the Israelis? "I heard one of the wounded soldiers say that the bomber, in spite of all he had done, should be treated as a human being. On the other hand, the sister of one of the injured was angry at me for giving the bomber the same care as her critically wounded sister."

Israeli tanks have encircled Jabel Fahm and enforced a curfew.

The Israeli high court has ruled against the expulsion of the families of the bombers to the Gaza area. The judges' decision cited the fact that the army had not shown sufficient proof that the two families were involved in aiding and abetting the bombers.

The Israeli police stated that the owner of Yoni's Diner, the employer of Sameh Laham, will be charged with hiring an illegal worker.

Clive Burleigh, WNS Middle East correspondent   *2:30 pm*

Behind me is a cemetery, but a very unusual one. This must be the only country in the world that has a cemetery for buses. This is the place in Israel where the buses go to die.

Remarkable as it may seem, the charred remains of the buses exploded by suicide bombers are not scrapped. Instead, these charred hulks are hauled to this large sandy stretch of land in a mountainous region of Israel. Here, in a lot the size of a soccer field, efforts continue to find personal possessions or human remains.

The latest arrival is the number 9 bus, site of the bomb explosion on Highway 1. It's the black skeleton over there, with only a hint of its original roof. Standing next to me is the bus company mechanic who manages this metal graveyard. He is, as you will hear, painfully aware of the human stories behind the twisted metal.

"Early this morning three volunteers arrived to search for any

body part that might have been overlooked at the scene of the explosion. You know, Jewish law requires burial of every part of a human being, even if it is pieces of skin."

Was anything found?

"One of the volunteers found a large photograph. Hard to believe paper could survive those flames—the paper clip had melted. Probably the clip held other papers or photos. Who knows? It was stuck under the mechanism that opens the back door."

What was it a picture of?

"I don't know. They didn't tell me."

This is a tough job. Have you thought of leaving the bus company?

"My father and grandfather were bus drivers and mechanics, but I hope my son chooses another career. After all, it's not the world it used to be, is it?"

No, I'd have to agree with you, and I think our viewers would also. This is Clive Burleigh for WNS, reporting from somewhere in Israel.

2:45 PM **Vera Brodsky** Orthopedic ward—room 414, Hadarim Hospital

"Vera, can you hear me? Squeeze my hand, please."

I hear but I can't get my body to do what I want it to do, squeeze his hand, talk to him, that's what I want the most—to talk to him. Lines of pain are shooting from my shoulder down my arm.

Silence. Far away past the numb edges of my body I hear a machine beeping. I can't move. Am I paralyzed? No way to know. Footsteps. Help me, please.

Rubber-soled steps moving near me. The nurse's voice. "Vera, I'm going to give you a pill. It will help the pain go away."

I open my mouth. She puts it on my tongue and then places a cup of water near my lips. I swallow the pill with some water.

The fire pain in my shoulders and legs moves away and away to nothing. My legs and arms are patted by a stream of cool air moving through the inside of my body.

"Feeling better?" a woman's voice asks.

The stones that press against my eyes are lifted and the throbbing ends.

The darkness fades. . . . I open my eyes.

"Dan?"

He bends over and kisses me. "Do you hear my heart? It's beating with yours. You'll live, Vera, you'll live. As long as I'm alive, you'll be alive. You're like a chamber of my heart. Do you hear me?"

I cry and cry and cry. How can I cry if my face is frozen? Where are the tears coming from, where is the sound I'm making coming from? The explosion. The bodies next to me, twisted and bleeding. The bodies that didn't look like human beings. Parts of bodies, torn-apart dolls with only hands and necks. People burning. People screaming. The smell, the terrible smell. Flesh being burned. Even animals don't die this way. Afraid no one would find me. Afraid I would die.

"Aagh." A strange voice with no words. I can't move. My body belongs to someone else.

I don't see Dan. He is a shape near me, that's all. In my head I want to say, You're the only person I love. I can't get the words out. They're in a word box in the middle of my brain, and that hurts so much I want to scream. I choke, can't get air into me. So many things to tell him. Now. Before I die. Everything hurts so much.

Lidia Adler Orthopedic ward—room 414, Hadarim Hospital   *3:05 PM*

I've got my camera. I tiptoe around her bed, clicking from every angle. The other bed is empty again, but I still don't want to make noise. She is bandaged and hooked up to all the machines, the IV in her arm. Pictures of my best friend. What will she look like after this? What will she be like? Terrified of going out, scared of being on her own, always dreaming of the explosion? Will her leg heal? Her arm? Will she be able to work, to study?

She would kill me if she saw me taking these pictures. "Lidia, no one knows this, but I'm the vainest person you'll ever meet," she told me once. She is also the most beautiful person I ever met.

Her parents are just as she described them. She's a mixture of them. Actually she looks more like her father. She probably wouldn't want to hear that. They don't even suspect that I know everything about them. I tell them I am taking photographs for an album about the number 9 bus explosion. They stare at me strangely. They think it's too horrible for anyone to keep a record of this.

They stared at Dan in his uniform, at me, at Baruch when he came into the room. Do we look Israeli, different from what they imagined? They looked away when Dan kissed Vera. I photographed it, the tall soldier leaning over the bed of a patient who can barely be seen for all the tubes and bandages. Are they embarrassed when they see real love?

Vera, you're a part of me, my sister. I never said it to you. Can you hear me, Vera? In your dream, can you hear me?

The nurse comes in. Goodbye for now. In a little while I'll be back.

3:05 PM **Sameh Laham**, security prisoner 0593 Surgical ward—Isolation, Hadarim Hospital

POLICE OFFICER: Who sent you?

SAMEH LAHAM: I came on my own.

POLICE OFFICER: If you did this on your own, how come you're not dead?

Prisoner does not respond to the question.

POLICE OFFICER: Do you know how the bus exploded?

SAMEH LAHAM: Did you see my injuries? I have twelve stitches in my neck.

POLICE OFFICER: But you're alive. How do you explain that?

SAMEH LAHAM: It is the will of Allah.

POLICE OFFICER: Is it the will of Allah to kill innocent women and children?

SAMEH LAHAM: Why do you ask me? Ask someone who is more learned than me.

POLICE OFFICER: But you have memorized parts of the Koran. That makes you learned, doesn't it?

SAMEH LAHAM: You are not Muslim. What do you know about the Koran?

POLICE OFFICER: I know that it is full of wise sayings and teachings and that it teaches not to kill the innocent. Not to murder Muslims or non-Muslims. That is forbidden, isn't it?

SAMEH LAHAM: It depends if there is a holier cause, something greater than life.

POLICE OFFICER: What is greater than life?

SAMEH LAHAM: The land, our land, that is a cause greater than life.

POLICE OFFICER: Is the land worth killing mothers and babies?

SAMEH LAHAM: Did they die?

POLICE OFFICER: Who?

SAMEH LAHAM: The two women and the baby? The two Arab women sitting in the back, one held a baby.

POLICE OFFICER: They died. Did you know them?

Prisoner does not respond to the question.

POLICE OFFICER: I'll ask you again—did you know them?

SAMEH LAHAM: No! No! No! I didn't know them. I didn't know anyone on the bus. I didn't know there would be Arab mothers on the bus. I didn't know there would be Arab babies on the bus. They didn't tell me.

POLICE OFFICER: Who didn't tell you?

Prisoner does not respond to the question.

POLICE OFFICER: Sameh, *who* didn't tell you that there would be nothing left of those bodies to identify? Identification had to be made from skin and teeth. What are the names of the men who didn't tell you that?

SAMEH LAHAM: They didn't tell me their names. I met them twice, just twice. The second time, it was the last time, I made the video. They promised me that my mother would receive money, enough money to buy some land and to pay for my brothers' and sisters' education. They swore on the Koran. I think one of their names was Issam, but I'm not sure.

POLICE OFFICER: And what did Omar Joulani have to do with all of this?

SAMEH LAHAM: He took me to them. He brought me there.

POLICE OFFICER: How did you know him?

SAMEH LAHAM: We knew each other from school. Our village is small and so is Jabel Fahm. The school for both our villages is in Jabel Fahm. He also worked illegally.

POLICE OFFICER: Not anymore.

SAMEH LAHAM: I think I saw him.

POLICE OFFICER: Saw who?

The prisoner's heart monitor indicated irregular heartbeat. Medical intervention was requested. The interrogation was ended. Interrogation tape was delivered to Security Services.

6:00 PM **Baruch Ben Tov** Kibbutz Broshim, Judean Hills

Tidal waves of panic batter me. It is insane, without reason and out of my control. Peace and quiet around me. Only I am being chased by dogs, blinded by searchlights, huddling in a sewer. I move my chair near the window and sit there. I can only hope the cool evening air and the view of the fields will calm me. My body aches with fatigue, but if I give in to my tiredness, if I lie down on my bed, *they* will come. An old man like me cannot run anymore. I will not survive *them* a second time.

I know there are no more Nazis. I am not an insane idiot. I know that all this was in my past. But my past and present run together like a clock out of order. The doctor has told me many times that my fear is a result of what I went through. My head tells me he is right, but then my throat constricts and my heart pounds in my ears and my bed sheet is drenched with sweat. No reasonable explanation can stop my terror.

I take a pill and try to rest in my chair.

People think because I am alive, because I survived, I am brave. That is not true. I am a fearful person. I always have been. As a boy I was very shy and timid. During my school years I was prepared to walk an extra hour to avoid a bully.

Of the two of us it was Rachel who was the brave one. When I met her, I knew immediately she would change my life. We weren't even twenty, but we knew our lives would be lived together. She was so open, so totally happy. I could not get over the fact that she found me interesting, that she liked to be with me. She was studying music and would insist I come along with her to a concert or a choir rehearsal. She teased me for being so quiet. You must laugh more, you're much too serious, she said. And I did laugh more after we married. Friends said I'd become a different person.

This fear and panic is something I have not experienced for several years. Only one explanation—Thomas Wanninger. I am terrified I will be hospitalized, the way I was when I first came to Israel.

I live two lives. One life is the world of memory, the other life is outside my head, here at the kibbutz. I am the Baruch people pass and nod *shalom* to, the gardener who grows wonderful roses and is praised for their beauty, the *meshugeneh*, the ancient one who can listen to Beethoven for hours. My world today is as narrow as that attic was.

This boy, this German volunteer, Thomas Wanninger, has upset the orderly balance of my life. I know he is not to blame, but I am angry. If I do not have order in my life, I will not survive.

The evening light illuminates the window box, and the red and pink geraniums are full and extravagant. I would never have thought I'd become a gardener—I was such a city person. But that was then.

Tomorrow I will have to be at the hospital again. What will I say to Ilse Wanninger? Tell her my life story? Retell my suffering? I saw her staring at my arm, at the number. Surely she knows what it is. When her son comes out of his coma, she will tell him about me. What I am. I cannot.

She is certain I will become his friend. After all, the world says that a Holocaust survivor should be grateful that the younger generation wants to know the truth. When you know the truth, you can repent. Thomas is here for something, and I will be sucked into it. Yes, I, Baruch, will unravel some German's last will and testament.

Staring at the orderly rows of sunflowers, I admit to a truth that surprises me. I have a tenderness for this Thomas, this boy who came here because of his conscience. His mother cries and says, I have only one son, no husband, it is too dangerous here.

We'll have to wait until he recovers, I tell her. When he feels stronger, when he can talk, you can discuss it with him.

But what do *you* think? she asks. You have been through so many things. Surely you know I'm right. It is mad to stay in this hell.

But he had a reason, I say.

That is not important anymore. Too many people, she says, have died for one truth or another.

There is nothing I can say.

TUESDAY, APRIL 11

Dr. Ibrahim Stitti 14 Khirbet Salih Street, Beit el E'Nab,
Palestinian Authority

The apartment is quiet, only the hum of the refrigerator in the kitchen. I make myself a cup of coffee and sit down at the kitchen table. Yesterday's evening newspaper is lying folded on the table. I can see that Nadine hasn't even opened it. She is right—what is there to read? Every day our newspapers and the Israeli newspapers carry the same mixture of hate and violence, the same headlines of distrust and accusations. All this and photographs, as if the words aren't enough. Front page and centerfold studded with pictures of dismembered bodies, sobbing kids, grieving parents, Arab mothers holding sick babies, waiting at the barricades to pass through and travel to Hadarim or some other hospital on the Israeli side of the border.

Bobby, our old Labrador, pads into the kitchen and nuzzles up to my leg. "Have a good day, Bobby. Take care of the girls and Nadine, okay?" I pat his head. I look at my watch. No time to linger. Who knows how long I'll have to wait at the checkpoints today.

It is getting late. I leave my coffee cup in the sink and toss the folded newspaper into the garbage pail.

As I approach the checkpoint, I can see a mass of vehicles in the distance. Something must have happened here. There are tank transporters, jeeps, Border Police, regular police. I'm careful not to speed. Who knows what they're looking for—no sense in drawing attention to myself.

Even driving slowly I reach the first checkpoint in less than five minutes. A series of thick concrete blocks straddle the width of the road. They look like doors except there are no hinges or keyholes. There are three soldiers. Two are leaning against the blocks. They're yawning but their rifles are ready.

It's early. Even so a dozen men are waiting in a line at the side of the road. They have their green and orange ID cards in their hands. I park my car on a narrow ledge near the barricade. I lock the doors. There are other cars parked here, all with Palestinian license plates, all forbidden to enter Israel.

I get into line. Some of the men recognize me and nod. They know I'm a doctor. They move aside and let me go ahead. I'm uncomfortable about this but grateful. The movement in the line makes the soldier look up. "Don't push your way forward!" he shouts at me. I retreat a few steps. It would not be smart to get this young soldier angry. Chances are he has been manning this checkpoint since midnight, maybe longer. His eyes are red and he is unshaven.

I'm standing a short distance behind a middle-aged man. He looks familiar.

"How do I know you have to appear in court?" the soldier asks him.

The man opens his briefcase and shows the soldier a file. "See, this is the case, and here is my name as the defending lawyer. It is a simple case of a building violation. Look," he says, opening the file, "this is the address of the Jerusalem municipal court."

Now I remember the man. He is a well-known Palestinian lawyer who practices in Palestinian and Israeli courts.

"And this case will be settled today—you will return this evening?"

"Inshallah," says the lawyer. He shrugs his shoulders in resignation. Who knows what will be decided and when? Only Allah knows. He turns around and looks at me and winks, as if saying, You know what I'm talking about, don't you?

"Put your briefcase on the ground and take off your jacket and open up your shirt."

The lawyer does exactly as he is told. The soldier spills the contents of the briefcase on the ground. Sandy dirt covers the typewritten pages. Then he frisks the lawyer's body under the opened white shirt and runs his hand around the belt of the pants.

"You can go."

Coming from the direction of the village is a water tanker. It's old, and as it drives over the potholes in the road it lurches from side to side. The soldiers order the men in line to push the concrete blocks aside so the tanker can get through. There's nothing more precious than water.

My turn.

"Why are you going to Jerusalem?"

"I'm a doctor at Hadarim Hospital, working in the intensive care unit."

"Sure, and I'm an alligator swimming in the Amazon River."

"Here are my identity papers and my hospital card."

He glances at what I hand over to him. I can see he is able to read the Arabic on my identity card. He looks intently at my photograph and then at me.

"Same person," I say.

"Every one of you has a mustache. How do I know you're a doctor?" he says.

I point to my hospital card. "You can see I am wearing a white coat in the hospital photograph. It says 'Doctor.'"

"An Arab doctor in a Jewish hospital—you really want me to believe that? Maybe you work in a garage and a doctor lost this card, or you stole it. How do I know?"

"Look, I know you have to check me out, so I'll make it easy for you. Call this number. It's a doctor in the ICU, he works with me. He'll verify who I am." I take a piece of paper out of my wallet with Razine's cell phone number.

"Give me your phone."

I hand him my cell phone and the piece of paper.

He dials. I'm lucky, Dr. Shmuel Razine hasn't turned off his phone. I stand there listening to a verbal Ping-Pong match about my identity. The soldier hands the phone back to me.

"Okay, shirt off and open up the belt."

I do as I am told. I shove my resentment and anger as far down into my body as I can. The worst thing would be for this young man to see irritation or anger on my face. Quiet obedience will reassure him that he is doing his job correctly.

He touches every part of my body. "No explosives today, eh, Doc?" I don't answer. "Okay, get dressed. I'm finished."

I circle around the concrete blocks and walk down the dirt road to the next checkpoint. Two months ago, five Israeli soldiers and three civilians were ambushed and killed here. There are still wreaths of dried flowers and stubs of memorial candles scattered over the ground. Next, if I'm lucky, I'll pick up an Israeli taxi and get to the hospital on time. There is a coma case, a German teenager who was in the bus explosion, waiting for me in the ICU.

I reach the second barricade of concrete blocks and the final checkpoint I have to get through. I look at my watch. 8:30 A.M. Almost three hours since I left home. I approach.

"What's your name?" the soldier asks.

8:30 AM **Sameh Laham**, security prisoner 0593 Surgical ward— Isolation, Hadarim Hospital

My leg and arm hurt. The plastic cuffs cut into my skin. I told them yesterday I can't even piss the right way because I can't move my body onto the bedpan. They don't care. The policeman who speaks Arabic is worse than the other one. He curses me all the time.

They look at my face and they can see I'm in pain. They don't care. The nurse is okay, though, and the doctors. They've got Arab doctors here. I wish they'd give me an Arab doctor. I'd tell him how I saw the woman with her baby, just like my mother. I saw them at the back and I didn't touch the switch. I'll swear to them I didn't. I let the backpack slip off. I didn't set off anything. They're smart, they have laboratories with microscopes and they can see fingerprints. The police and the Special Security agents—they're all over the place. The agents don't wear uniforms, they disguise themselves as Palestinians or Israeli Arabs so you never know who you're talking to. The police, the agents, even those religious people who say what they collect is for burial, pick up everything from the ground. Whatever they find on the bus they take to a special place where they have all sorts of equipment, more than the Americans have. They're smart, these people, all of them. They know I didn't blow up the bus. It was the driver of the yellow van. It was Omar.

"You know, I don't hate Jews," I tell them.

"So what are you trying to say, Sameh?"

"That you should go easy on me. You know all about me, I'm not a terrorist. You won't find my name on any of the lists of those people. I made a mistake—I believed it was only Jews who would die. You Israelis have a country, we don't. We also deserve a country."

"A minute ago, Sameh, you said you don't hate Jews, and now you're saying you wanted to kill them."

"No, not kill, just show the world we're also entitled to freedom."

"By killing an Arab woman and her baby, by murdering an Arab high school student?"

"You're confusing me. You're trying to get me to say things that aren't the truth."

"Actually it's the truth we want to hear."

"Don't put me in jail and I will tell you whatever you want to hear. I promise."

The policeman who curses looks at me. "Poor Sameh," he says, and mutters in Arabic.

I turn my face to the wall. Everything is over.

"What did you say to him?" asks the other policeman.

"I told little Sameh," the Arab-speaking policeman answers, "to each his fate."

10:15 AM **Baruch Ben Tov** Intensive care unit—Neurology, Hadarim Hospital

Doctor Stitti is inside doing tests on Tommi. He's been very sympathetic and very kind to Ilse Wanninger. I told her I will be here this morning so she can rest a bit. I still haven't spoken to Thomas.

The social worker met me a few minutes ago and gave me Tommi's backpack. It was recovered by the rescue crew and brought to the hospital. If I get a chance to be with him, I'll take it with me. If his eyes are open and he recognizes it, I'm sure it will make a difference to how he feels.

Yesterday the doctor came in every few hours to see if there was any change in Tommi's coma. Usually he had a little joke for me. Today he hurried in, carrying many reports and x-rays. He looked angry and only nodded at me. I did not stop him to ask about Tommi.

I am alone in the waiting room. Dan and Lidia are in Vera's room on the fourth floor. Lidia has become the documenter of this event. She does not shy away from photographing anything, no matter how distressing. "Someone has to show how it was," she says. Vera's parents and Tommi's mother are astounded. They cannot understand her courage or her curiosity. It is hard for all of them. This is a country that consumes its inhabitants. There is no desert island to escape to.

Yesterday I went to see Vera. Her beautiful hands, her long fingers, the nail polish still on her fingernails. I invited her parents to have coffee with me at the kibbutz one afternoon.

"I can't leave her, even for a minute," Vera's mother said. "I'll come when this is all over."

"*This*, as you call it," the father said to her, "will never end."

In the waiting rooms and in the cafeteria, Ilse and Vera's parents have endless discussions about taking their children away from here. They do not ask me what I think.

Why must every generation carry the story of the generations before? The young should start life with no history, no old stories. Vera's parents are here with their story, and Tommi's mother, and the memory story of his father. Now I am part of the story, and Dan, and Lidia, and also the Palestinian boy, the suicide bomber. Like tangled string when you pull at it, it gets tighter.

Patient: Thomas Wanninger   *11:00 AM*
Examining Physician: Dr. Ibrahim Stitti

Motor Response:	Follows simple commands—Score: 6
	Localizes pain, pulls away from examiner's hand when pinched—Score: 5
	Abnormal extension, body semirigid when pinched—Score: 5
Eye Opening:	Spontaneous—Opens eyes on own, keeps them open—Score: 6
	Voice—Opens eyes to command even in whispered voice—Score: 7
Verbal Response (Talking):	Orientation—can tell who he is, where, month and year, some sporadic confusion and hallucinations—Score: 6
Assessment:	Satisfactory improvement

11:15 AM   **Thomas Wanninger** Intensive care unit–Neurology, Hadarim Hospital

I am in the train without windows. I was here before. I am going somewhere I don't want to go. To visit Opa Hans? The people in their dirty-smelling coats are pushing me against the wooden slats of the railroad car. Someone is pinching me, talking to me. If I open my eyes, they will know I am alive. I must pretend to be dead. Someone's breath over my face. The brakes screech loudly, and the train jerks to a halt. I am thrown backward and forward and forward and backward. The people disappear from the railroad car. How? No one rolled open the door. Are they on a bus? Now I've fallen and there is a burning smell. A woman says I'm safe. You are safe, Tommi. Do not be afraid.

La-le-lu, nur der Mann im Mond schaut zu *the woman is singing,* wenn die kleinen Babys schlafen, drum schlaf auch du. La-le-lu. *Mutti's special song for me. Why is Mutti here in the railroad car? Will she die with me? The song doesn't stop, the sweet song. I am little, in my room.* Only the man in the moon watches when all the little babies sleep, so you sleep too. *Papa has come from his hospital bed and is tucking the blanket around me. . . .* Vor dem Bettchen steh'n zwei Schuh' . . . *and he'll see near my bed my pair of shoes. Someone is pulling my legs. I won't leave. I won't get off the train. If I get off, I will die. Mutti, Mutti.*

11:15 AM   **Vera Brodsky** Orthopedic ward–room 414, Hadarim Hospital

A light is shining in my face, pushing my eyes open. I want a mirror. I don't want anyone to see me until I have a mirror. Why are there so many tubes? Will I have to walk in the street with them? I feel something covering my face. How ugly am I? How ugly will I be? Forever?

Dan. Dan. I think I see his shoulders. What is he doing here in the middle of my pain? Don't go away. I love you. Is it in my head or am I saying it? Do you hear me? Do you?

The people in the room, the shapes, are swaying, turning, like a carousel. Mama, Papa, Lidia, dear Baruch. Mama and Papa are holding hands. Papa who taught me the multiplication tables, Mama who showed me how to peel an apple in a spiral that never broke . . .

I am running down a slope of fire. No matter how fast I run, it burns my legs, my hands, my stomach. Dan, you're a soldier—can't you help me? Put out the fire, Dan, please. Don't leave me . . . don't leave me like Sergei. Don't die.

Will you die, Dan? Dear Irena, I am writing this letter because very soon my hands will explode. Be brave. Go where your heart tells you to go and stay where your heart feels best. I will always love you, little sister. You are beautiful, my little sister. I will be your ugly sister. They will put me in a dark room like the bad witch in a fairy tale.

I know now how much I love Papa and how much he loves me. Mama, I didn't know. I love you both. I can be Verushka to both of you. Remember me when I am cinders and ashes. The light is in my eyes again. *Papa, before these flames swallow me up, are you watching me spin?*

Baruch Ben Tov Waiting room, intensive care unit—Neurology, Hadarim Hospital   *11:15 AM*

This is the second day Dr. Stitti has asked me to have my blood pressure checked. The nurses in the unit told him I was under some stress, he explained to me. He is concerned. He suggests a tranquilizer. I tell him the doctor at the kibbutz has given me tranquilizers. I tell him the name. I want you to take something a bit stronger, he says. I agree. I think I am losing my sanity, and that is forbidden. I must stay sane. Even then, at that time, I did not become a skeletal madman embracing my end and blabbering grateful thanks to the God who was hovering above the black smoke of the crematorium.

He jots the figures down and tells me to give it to my doctor at the kibbutz.

SYS 192   DIA 105   PULSE 68/min

3:00 PM Thomas Wanninger Intensive care unit—Neurology, Hadarim Hospital

The old man is still sitting next to my bed. He was here with Mutti. Before. I don't remember when. He is speaking. I watch his lips move but I can't hear the words. What are you saying, old man? I can't move my head. The ringing in my ears is as loud as church bells. I have so many tubes. When there's less pain, I talk in my head. I think of Papa, the cancer pain. I didn't help him much. I wish he were still alive. I would tell him I know how bad pain is.

Stupid me, I feel cold snow and smell burning rubber. Where am I? In Berlin, in a bus? Will I have legs? And girls . . . Christina . . . will I be with girls?

I open my eyes. I hear the old man. In German. Talking German. I can't believe it.

He leans forward in his chair. "I'm sorry, I was talking in German and hoping you'd open your eyes. Your mother has gone to the kibbutz to rest a few hours. I am Baruch Ben Tov, from Kibbutz Broshim. I'm the head gardener."

I can't put this together. The kibbutz gardener, but he speaks German. Upside down, the world has turned upside down.

A sound, the beginning of the word for "girl." I try to say it, but nothing comes out.

"Yes, the girl who picked you up. Vera."

Nod, Tommi. Show you are trying to understand.

"She's on another floor. She'll be all right. And I have something that I think will please you."

Nod again, Tommi.

He bends down. Because of the tubes and the pillows I can't see the floor. What is he doing?

He lifts up a backpack, dirty, ripped, torn, blue backpack—mine. I blink my eyes.

"Yes, Tommi, the police found it. Well, the zipper is gone and probably a lot of things that were in it, but still, here it is."

I make sounds. He jumps up from the chair.

"Please do not upset yourself. I'll get the nurse." He goes away.

He comes back. A nurse with him. Looks at the tubes and presses something. The old man talks and talks. In German.

"There was an explosion on the bus. You were unconscious and your body has many fractures and bruises."

This old man . . . why is he so certain of what he's telling me? The burning smell in my nose. The screams. Blood, blood, blood. Pieces of my body. I. Die. Coming here . . . now . . . nothing. Opa's photographs—where . . . where? It's a terrible riddle.

"Your mother has told me why you're here."

I try to make the sound.

"Opa. Yes, I know, Tommi. Your mother has told me. I know what you want to find out."

Am I crying? Is this me? I can't feel. I can't move my head. No . . . not . . . see me crying.

"Please don't cry. I promise to look for your grandfather's photographs."

I move my head as much as I can. I try to sit up. . . . I must . . . about Opa Hans before I die. I can move one of my fingers. I make the sign of the cross.

"No, you won't. You won't die. Everything will be all right."

Every day in the camp, every single day, I pieced together another one of Professor Kleist's lectures, one physics theorem after another, one proof after another. When I had finished, I started all over again. This way I kept myself from falling into the black unknown. My daily routine began with reconstructing my first-year notebook—Physics I.

While I cleaned out the bathrooms, I posed questions that I was forced to answer. Sharp, my mind must remain sharp or I will not survive. I had to survive. I had to remain sane. Do eye and brain perform the same functions? Why do we see objects that are not there? These were the two questions I returned to every day. I answered with the scientific facts I had learned from Kleist. The velocity of light and the delay in the nervous messages reaching the brain cause us to see the past though we think we are seeing the present. The present was banished to my peripheral vision. I did not see the rows of prisoners led to the showers, I did not see those who fell and froze in the fields. That was on the outskirts of my sight—just as Professor Kleist had said. I embraced only the past.

1. White light contains all the colors of the spectrum.
2. The brain discerns stillness, absence of movement.
3. The camera can record; it cannot explain.

I recalled far more than that, but I would always stop there. If I lived through the night, there would be a next day. I needed material to survive the next day. I always stopped at "The camera can record; it cannot explain."

Vladek found a copy of *Alice in Wonderland* under the third-floor landing. "I didn't know Lewis Carroll lived in a Jewish ghetto." We all laughed. We laughed, I remember that.

Rachel was a true idealist. We were always having fights

about the rights of the majority and the rights of the minority. What disturbed her was the power of the majority to impose its will. I hear her voice, how triumphant she was when she won a political argument, how red her cheeks became. What a burden memory is.

I lift the glass of water to my lips and swallow the second pill Dr. Stitti gave me.

Hitler poisoned the Jewish people. Death was a sure thing, but he and his henchmen dangled the possibility of life in front of the poor Jews. Some Jews. He caused them to turn against one another, brother hating brother, friend betraying friend, mothers choosing between their children. The beauty of Jewish life turned ugly. No prayer, no benediction, no psalm would ever hold the same meaning.

Is the span of one's life predetermined?

Pavel and Klara, Irka, Tadeusz, Rachel.

And Thomas and Vera.

I have asked the doctor at the kibbutz, many times, to explain the difference between a night memory and a day memory. Doctor, tell me, how am I able to go about my tasks during the day not thinking once about that time, but at night it rises like a monster from the sea? It is so terrifying that I must sleep with a light on. He gives me pills because he has no answer.

I still have that piece of paper I carried out of hell: on it my scribbled drawing of where we buried them. Probably all those buildings and yards disappeared in the bombardments. Probable, possible—all life and death a question mark. And Thomas's grandfather, a question mark I'll look for in the files of Yad Vashem. Will I give him an answer?

I know now that on September 21, 1939, a week before Poland's surrender, Reinhard Heydrich, chief of the German Security Police and Security Service, dispatched an express letter to his Special Action Squads in Poland informing them of the measures to be taken against Jews there. We were to stay home between nine P.M. and five A.M. We must wear the Star of David at all times. Everything we owned was to be declared.

May 1940. Holland fell to the Germans.

The restrictive measures made me into an animal. It was the beginning of everything I became afterward—suspicious, secretive, cynical, pessimistic. I was the prey facing the hunters. All of us in the attic were prey. Vladek, Pavel, Klara, Uncle Mauritz, Rachel, even our baby.

Vladek was like a brother to me. We were like twins, except he had his Zionism, his dream, his Utopian country. Would you believe, Vladek, I am the one living here, and you are the soil under the Auschwitz grass? In my heart you remain my brother. You knew me the best. You saw to what depths I could sink.

From the attic window I saw the vehicles and cavalry. Always heavy artillery. Rachel lived in continual panic. The rumble of the tanks on the cobblestones made her break out in a cold sweat. All her intellectual resources were of no help. The irrationality of the Germans made her irrational. I couldn't blame her. But one of us had to stay calm—it was the only way we would survive.

We were still managing to feed the little one. Daniel. Daniel, who had survived the lion's den. He slept a great deal. Maybe nature was helping him to forget his hunger. No, he was still small and sleep was his job. That was what he had to do to grow. I tried to think of him as a young man. The thought of a future would keep my mind sharp.

The punishment for everything was death. Nothing was too trivial. Only hiding would save us. Maybe escape, but that didn't look possible. We weren't sure which of the Polish neighbors we could trust. With the bit of first aid knowledge I had, I took care of the landlord's son when he had an eye infection. The landlord kissed my hand. He swore on his mother's grave he would never betray us. He could have sworn on his whole family tree, I didn't believe him.

Our nerves were frayed almost to the breaking point. The

baby cried more and more each day. Rachel had no more milk to nurse him. The streets were silent with death and the curfew. The landlord said the baby's crying could be heard from the street.

Vladek found someone who would take us to the woods. Rachel swore she had no strength to be a partisan—the only strength she had she saved for the little one. The patrols and search parties were becoming more frequent. From the narrow window I could see only the tops of their hats, their vehicles, their shadows.

Vladek said time was running out.

Terrible news. Tomorrow two German captains would be taking over the first-floor apartment. "These days you know how it is," the landlord said in his street-market Polish. He made a gesture with his fingers, as if he were counting coins. And the Poles say that *Jews* live only for money!

We gave Vladek money to pass along to the Polish partisans. Rachel cried all the time now. The baby mewled like a hungry kitten. The landlord said we had to leave by Wednesday. And would I be good enough to look at his son's eye before I went?

I made up my mind we would survive. I repeated it. "Survive, survive, survive." I made Rachel repeat it. It was our litany.

More Germans moved into the house. One day we heard them on the second and third floors. We were the only Jews left in the house. Like rats we lived under the roof.

The Germans liked to sing. I hoped it would cover up the baby's cries.

It was arranged. Vladek passed the money. We were to leave the next day.

Then the baby became feverish. Vladek kept telling me the baby's howling was going to get us all killed. Rachel sat on the floor rocking the baby. I was the only one she'd talk to. "What does Vladek want me to do? What is he saying? Tell me." I knew what Vladek was saying, but I didn't have the courage to tell her.

I paid the landlord to bring us a bottle of slivovitz. I didn't want her to hear or see what I was going to have to do. I prepared a glassful and left the bottle near her mattress. Rachel, drink it. She looked at me. I kissed her and said Yes, drink, it will help you sleep. Vladek took the baby out of her arms when she fell asleep. She was so tired, so undernourished, that she fell asleep without drinking the liquor.

There was a narrow opening behind the attic wall, behind the beds where we slept. Vladek, my best friend. Vladek, I will never forget you.

"I will do it," I said. I took the baby out of Vladek's arms. I took my pillow, a soft goose-down pillow, and I placed it over my son's face. As weak as he was, he struggled. His fingers curled and uncurled, he gurgled, he peed in my hands, he flung his legs out, what a strong boy he would have grown up to be. He died in the dark space behind the wall.

She never told me she had a vial of potassium cyanide. When had she lost hope and prepared her death? Before Daniel's death, when she couldn't nurse him anymore, or after I told her what I had done? Was it then that she decided on suicide? Who sold it to her? I am sure it was the landlord.

Vladek and I left for the woods after the patrol passed our street.

God put Abraham to the test. He said, "Take your son, your favored one, Isaac, whom you love, and offer him as a burnt offering." Abraham took the wood for the burnt offering and put it on his son. He himself took the firestone and the knife. Then Isaac said to his father, Abraham, "Here are the firestone and the wood, but where is the sheep for the burnt offering?"

Abraham did not answer. Because there is no answer for that question.

He bound his son. He laid him on the altar he had made.

The altar God had commanded that he build in the ghetto, behind the wall in the roof, behind his bed where he slept with his wife. The Lord called to him from heaven, "Abraham, Abraham." And he answered, "Here I am." But this time, in the ghetto, with a soft pillow, God did not stay the father's hand from slaughtering his child.

Tomorrow is Wednesday. So many years, and here it is another Wednesday in my life. I must admit to the horrible fact—discovering even one hideous act of Opa Hans Wanninger would be my sweet release. It was the Nazis who turned me into a monster. Maybe the discovery of his evil will free me from *my* evil. As for Thomas and his mother, they are prepared for the worst.

I walk toward the guest hostel, to Thomas's room, to speak with his mother.

Alex Ushakov Cafeteria, Hadarim Hospital   4:15 PM

I am such a clever person, a physicist with a reputation, head of the physics department at Mechnikov University, so why did I insist that everything be *my* way? Vera had changed, she was changing under my very eyes in Odessa, and I never saw it. She wanted to be independent, she wanted me to understand her, she wanted my love.

Even now, in the burning hell of her pain, she loves. She whispers about Irena, and Lidia, and Dan, and Sergei. Does Dan hear her say Sergei's name? Does he know about him?

When her eyes opened, she received me back into her heart. I haven't heard her say "Papa" that way for years. Nothing stays the same, isn't that what we physicists say? Except love, of course.

The wall above her desk is covered with postcards of Odessa. There is a sweeping view of the Black Sea, an old postcard of the Moblish Erulim Synagogue, and a black-and-white card of the famous Potemkin Steps. She has taped up family photos, Irena and Babushka, her mother, her friend Galina, her and Dan, us. I stand and look at these postcards and photos on the white wall.

Photographs are like a diary, a record of your life. This is Vera's life. But only part. I'm recording the part she will need to know about afterward. Other people should know it too. From the first minute I started carrying my camera to the hospital, taking pictures, I knew what I was meant to do. The first day I was ashamed, as if I were a Peeping Tom, a person enjoying the pain of other people, strangers. Now I think it's important.

I've got to find something in her room that will make her fight. There's a row of snapshots of flowers and trees thumbtacked across the wall. She borrowed my camera to take them. Then I remember the lilacs she planted and tended. She'd asked Baruch if lilacs would grow in Israel. Of course, he answered, and the best place for lilac bushes is in the cool air of the Judean Hills, or Safed, up north. Plant them in a garden here and you'll have success. Can you believe it, she said to me, I came to one of the few places in Israel where I can plant lilacs.

In another row, above the bookshelf with books in English and Hebrew and Russian, are more photographs: Vera and her sister ice-skating, the two of us rafting on the Jordan River, and Vera and Baruch Ben Tov standing in a field of sunflowers. There's Vera and Dan, arms around each other, in a circle of people singing. At the end of the row of photos, above her desk lamp, framed with silver foil paper, is a snapshot that must have been taken just before she left home. It is of her mother, Irena, and Babushka in Shevchenko Park, the ground covered with snow, in front of the obelisk.

I look at my watch. It's getting late. Where is the photograph of the lilacs? The photograph I developed and gave her? I open the long center drawer of her desk. There's a small white cardboard box, and under it a pile of letters and cards tied with a green satin ribbon. A photo slips out of the pile. Vera and a boy; he has blond curly hair, he's about her height, they're kissing. Who is he?

I sit down on the edge of her bed. On the night table is a small clay pot filled with dried rose petals. The scent is almost gone. Under the pot I see the photo of her and the lilacs.

This is what I will put next to her bed in the hospital.

Strange she hasn't told me about that blond boy. Has she told Dan?

I leave her room. It is a short walk to the small house on the edge of the sunflower field. I promised Baruch I would have tea with him. Me, instead of Vera.

The door is open. An aria floats out of the house into the spring air.

"Come in, come in," he says. "I know you'd rather hear something with castanets and guitars, but you'll have to put up with Bach."

"Baruch, really, I don't mind classical music."

"Lidia, you are one of the politest girls on this kibbutz."

"Sure, sure. And you're the best substitute grandfather a polite girl can have."

"I guess that makes us family, then."

Three years ago, when I first met Baruch, I saw the blue ink number on his arm. I have never said anything. I wouldn't know what to say. A man who had been part of the Holocaust, who had survived, it seemed impossible. I remember my father talking about the war and the concentration camps in Europe, but to meet someone . . .

"Maybe coffee this time, Lidia?"

"No, Baruch, tea, please. In honor of Vera." I take the

snapshot of the lilacs out of my shoulder bag. "I've decided to bring this to Vera in the hospital. She said they are a symbol of everything that's beautiful in life."

Baruch smiles. "I think they were one of the first things she planted. She bought a small-sized bush and I gave her a little section of garden for it. 'Can you imagine, Baruch,' she said, 'they told me in the nursery that lilacs are made for the Jerusalem climate, especially here, at the kibbutz. High and cool.'

"We'd never had a lilac bush, but she was stubborn about wanting something that reminded her of Odessa. She coaxed it to grow, the way a mother teaches a baby to walk. She never gave up." As he looks at the photo, the teakettle whistles. He gets up. "Yes, it will do her good."

He pours the tea into our cups and then brings a plate of cookies and a tray of small sandwiches from the tiny kitchenette.

"When I have tea with Vera, she usually brings her babushka's teapot and we brew our tea in that."

"Baruch, do you know anything about her life in Odessa?"

"Yes, she talks about her school, her friends, and the letters her grandmother writes her."

"No one else?"

"No. Who else?"

"Oh, I don't know. Maybe a boyfriend."

I sit opposite Baruch and wait for an answer. If she told anyone at all, it would be him. But he's lost in the arias of Bach and I can't ask any more. We listen to the music without speaking. Outside, the sunflowers begin to close. It is almost evening.

"Poor Thomas," I say, "just wanted to volunteer in Israel and look what happens to him."

He says nothing. But hearing Thomas's name upsets him. The hand that is holding the teacup shakes.

"Will you go to the hospital tomorrow?"

"I don't know, Lidia. I'm feeling a bit tired. This has been a difficult time for me. Well, I'm sure also for you."

"Yes. I still can't believe what's happened to Vera. And to all the people on the bus. Why? What for? Even when they get out of the hospital, they'll never be the same. Vera's mind is still on the bus. She talks about the smells, what she saw, it doesn't leave her. It's hard to understand hate."

I get up. "Thank you, Baruch. For the tea." I help him carry the tray and cups to the kitchen counter.

We stand by the door and look at the golden field. He puts his hand on my shoulder.

"She will love the photo of the lilacs, Lidia. If anything helps her to recover, it will be that. Only a sister would think of that."

Sameh Laham, security prisoner 0593 Surgical ward—Isolation, Hadarim Hospital   5:20 PM

I will forever be the coward, the traitor, the betrayer of my people. My nation. And now I have nothing to give my mother. She will not receive the money they promised. My brothers will be spat on. Terrible things will be done to me in jail. What Arab wishes a person like me to continue living?

I swore to the policemen that I am against bloodshed and killing. They laughed at me.

I took an oath on the holy Koran that I would commit this act of martyrdom. I failed. Why did that mother sit there, why did she rock the baby? Why? Why?

The policemen taunt me with the newspapers. They throw in my face the pictures of the dead, the little baby—Mervat, four months old—and her mother. I wanted to save them. I swear to Allah I did. Didn't I yell to them, *"Yalla, yalla?"* The words were in my head. I heard them. Hurry and get off the bus. Run away.

Yesterday the two policemen told me there's a room on this floor with a girl in it who is so badly burned, the doctors can't identify her. Think of that, Sameh. Your mother will look at you, she will recognize you. But not this girl. You did that, Sameh.

When her father finds her, he will come to seek revenge. But we won't let him. We are policemen. We will guard you so you can stand in court and tell your story. A *shaheed* who was afraid.

But it wasn't me. It was Omar. The Boss could tell them I was a good worker. No one listens to me.

8:00 PM **Thomas Wanninger** Intensive care unit–Neurology, Hadarim Hospital

I wake up. I can hear the radio at the nurses' station. It's very low, but I hear the beep-beep signal of the hourly news. I don't want to know about another explosion, more dead people. It's good the news is in Hebrew and I don't understand it. I can breathe now without the ventilator. It's becoming easier to talk.

Now I call the old man by his first name. He told me to.

"Baruch, please, the answer. I must have the answer for my father. What did Opa Hans do?" I was upset. I cried and I was ashamed that I cried. I wanted my mother. "Mutti, Mutti."

I really am crying for myself. I am so afraid. Every time I hear a door slam or another noise or someone raises his voice, I get scared. I am terrified to go out. What will I do when I'm better? Hide?

The nurse said, It is a good sign you are talking. The coma is a thing of the past. Dr. Stitti will check you again tomorrow morning. Don't worry, you are out of danger.

I don't remember what happened when the old man was in my room. My backpack is propped up against the wall. I won't let anyone move it. Did I tell him the name of Opa's battalion, that Opa disappeared, that we don't know where and when he died? No, how could I, I couldn't talk.

When Dr. Stitti was here, he said Herr Ben Tov isn't feeling well.

"It's my fault. I cry when he is here."

"Don't worry, Tommi, you're not to blame. He is under medical care."

"*Danke*. Thank you. I have something to ask you, Dr. Stitti."

"Sure, anything, Tommi."

"My mother wants to take me back to Germany the minute I can travel. What do you think?"

"About being able to travel?"

"No, whether I'd be a coward if I left." I don't tell him about how scared I am. Maybe he's guessed.

"No one could call you a coward, Tommi. Ever."

Vera's friend Lidia is here, together with Dan. What good friends she has. Lidia is crazy about photography. Every day she comes to take my picture, sometimes with my mother, or a nurse, or Dr. Stitti. Once she took my picture with the backpack. A souvenir from the bus, she said.

"I don't want any souvenir," I told her, but she took the picture anyway.

Now I ask her, "Do you think I look German, Lidia?"

"I never thought about it. Why, does it make a difference to you?"

"Yes. . . . *La-le-lu*," I sing. "*. . . Und die sind genauso müde, geh'n jetzt zur Ruh'. . . .*"

Weird to remember a lullaby. I close my eyes. Sleep. Nothing will happen to me anymore. I have to believe that.

Dan Oron Orthopedic ward—room 414, Hadarim Hospital   11:00 PM

"Hello, Verushka."

"Hello, Dan. Since when do you call me Verushka?"

"I like it, and it's part of you, your Odessa part."

"I don't like to think about Odessa."

"I slept in your room last night. I lay in your bed and looked at your pictures on the wall. All those photos—I wish I'd been with you when they were taken. What a waste of time, not being together."

"I—"

"Don't talk. I know how your whole body hurts. But you're alive, you're alive. And everyone needs you to get well. Most of all, I need you. I can't do anything without you. And Baruch needs you. You're his granddaughter, he says. And so does Lidia."

"Lidia keeps taking my picture. I don't want her to. It's sick to do it."

"She's found a real purpose. To tell the story of *this*, of what happened."

"But not of a victim, of someone bandaged. Who wants to look at that kind of photograph? Dan—"

"What is it, Vera?"

"I have these terrible dreams, really horrible. All the time."

"I told the nurse. She says it's normal, it's the way your mind gets rid of fear."

"I have to tell you something."

"What, Vera?"

"It's the most important thing I've ever told you."

She starts to cry.

"Don't worry about it. There's plenty of time. It's late. Maybe you should sleep. I'll be here tomorrow."

"You know I got you a birthday present."

"That's all? Is that what you wanted to tell me?"

"Yes. Well, not really, but . . ."

She closes her eyes. Her voice gets sleepy.

"Do you want to learn Russian, Dan?"

"Maybe. I thought you wanted to forget your Odessa past. But you know I'm not good with languages." I think she's asleep.

Then she whispers, "Dan, I'll tell you. . . ."

"Tell me what?"

"Sergei, his name was Sergei."

There is no more strength in her to talk.

THURSDAY, APRIL 13

I slept badly last night. The truth is I didn't sleep at all. I took another sleeping pill at three in the morning. This killing of people on the bus, this barbarism, has shattered my peace. My body trembles, and the slightest noise makes me jump. Lidia comes to me to tell me she is changing her life, Dan asks me if love is stronger than fear, Thomas begs me to help him keep his promise to his father. Baruch, tell me, each one says. Baruch, you are older, wiser, find the answer.

Yesterday I filled out the application form—Yad Vashem, Holocaust Martyrs' and Heroes' Remembrance Authority. How official everything becomes—history, death, events. Here is an authority that gives you permission to remember. I wonder if there is an authority that gives you permission to forget.

Archives. First name, last name, telephone. I did not write my concentration camp number. Purpose of research: I wrote *Hans Wanninger*. How should I explain this in the small space on the page? I went back to the counter. The archivist got up from his seat and looked at me questioningly.

"Yes?" he asked.

I explained who Hans Wanninger was and who his grandson, Thomas Wanninger, is. I described the boy's physical state, then I explained that he was to work with me at the kibbutz. I leaned forward over the counter. The archivist glanced at my arm, saw the blue-inked number. He said nothing. He wrote something on the application form. I do not know, I said, what the young man, Thomas Wanninger, will do with the information about his grandfather. I added, as if I were defending him, I do not think it is for a book or newspaper article. It is for personal use, for himself. I wrote the date and signed the form.

The archivist did not pry or ask unnecessary questions. Odd: After some ten minutes or so I began to feel comfortable. I waited patiently. The anxiety and tension left my body. In that cool, well-lit room I felt I was with old friends. I knew the ghosts there.

The archivist brought me a folder. I opened it and began to read. Reading the documents, the eyewitness reports, looking at the photographs, was like a slow walk past headstones in a cemetery. After I finished, I moved from the long table and sat in front of a computer. I pressed a button. Black-and-white photographs moved across the screen. One after the other. Some clear, some blurred, some from a distance, some leaving nothing to anyone's imagination. One after the other.

The facts in the pages I read comforted me. My face was reflected on the computer screen—I became part of the photographs. Well, I was, wasn't I? Here, of all places, where I had never expected it, a bit of my pain and loneliness eased away. A human being is a strange creature. A solitary nightmare is a hideous terror. The truth when shared with others is a balm.

All these names, all these stories, all these inhuman acts done just to stay alive, not to die, not to die. People like me. Berkowitz, Shirman, Lubovsky, Friedman, Kappelwitz, Heyman, Rabinowitz, Weissman, Klagsman, Spielman, Zisman, Brozrowski, Kannerman, and more and more. Hundreds, thousands, millions, I could never read all the names. Then a man with my name—another Guttman, another Benjamin Guttman. But he died in a gas chamber in Bergen-Belsen.

Gutt I changed to the Hebrew *Tov,* "good," but I did not translate the second part, *man.* Instead I chose the word for "son"—*Ben.* A good son. And for my first name—Baruch, I told myself, "Blessed." Blessed be the memory of the good son.

Remember, you are here for one purpose. Don't read more than you have to. Click past the photographs that are not relevant to Thomas Wanninger and his grandfather. I found nothing. I turned off the computer.

I drank a glass of water.

I opened another folder. I came to three photographs. These three photographs corresponded to the date, the place, and the number of Hans Wanninger's battalion. They matched the description of the photographs Ilse had written down for me. I had found part of the evidence. Now maybe there would be an explanation.

The photos were grainy black and white. They were taken from some distance, but it was clear what was happening. They were probably taken by an unknown partisan, maybe Jewish, maybe Polish. A man or woman who was willing to risk capture and death to document the *Ordnungspolizei* carrying out a massacre.

Why would someone send copies of these photographs to the family of the dead Hans Wanninger? Who had sent them? Someone like me, a survivor?

Officer Wanninger had disappeared from his battalion, from Poland, from the eastern front, so why send his family these pictures?

I turned to the folder again.

SUBJECT: Klibiski Massacre, Klibiski, Poland. August 3, 1942. Witness testimony given by Abraham Zeligman, February 11, 1955.

I was arrested on August 2 by the Gestapo. I was taken to the largest house in the Polish village of Klibiski. It was one of the houses in the area that belonged to a wealthy Polish count and had been taken over by the Gestapo.

All my belongings were taken from me: the keys to the safe house used by the local partisans, a pack of cigarettes, a photo of my children, even two caramel candies. I was suspected of being a courier for the Polish resistance. That I was also a Jew made my crime even more appalling.

I was locked in a solitary cell that had once been the wine cellar. A guard stood outside the door. They had forgotten to take my belt and shoelaces. It was a stupid mistake, but after thinking about it for an hour or so, I decided I would not give them the satisfaction of my suicide.

I observed the guard very carefully. He seemed bored. I wondered if he could be bribed. I struck up a conversation with him. He told me that a lot of scum like me were to be killed in the morning. All the villagers would be taken to the mill outside the village. Probably their bodies would be buried in the field or thrown into the river. All the inhabitants of Klibiski were going to be shot. He made it clear that I would be included in this killing.

I told him I knew where more partisans were hiding, partisans who had been recruited from Klibiski. He became excited and left. A half hour later he returned with a lieutenant. "The guard tells me you have some information," he said. I said yes and repeated my statement. He warned me that if my information was a ruse to try to escape, it wouldn't work. I told him I wasn't that courageous.

The next morning I was put into the back of a car. The lieutenant was the driver. There were just the two of us. We passed the thatched-roof houses of the village and then some fields, a small forest, and then the mill and a small river. There I saw three battalion trucks of the *Ordnungspolizei,* or as they were called, the Orpo, parked off to the side. The Reserve Police had lined up the villagers in rows. But just the women, children, and old people. The able-bodied men were digging long pits. The lieutenant pushed me forward, and we walked toward the officer in charge.

The officer was addressing the policemen. I cannot testify to everything he said. I heard only part of his orders: "If you are not able to perform this act, if the task is too difficult, you can step away."

As we got nearer, I could see the officer's rank. He was a major.

"I'm Lieutenant Brunn, Gestapo." The lieutenant did not comment on what the major had said to the battalion. I can say this because I am sure he did not hear it. To a Gestapo officer that statement would have been treason.

"Major Schnitke, Reserve Police."

"This piece of partisan garbage says there are one or two partisans hiding in the mill building. Give me one of your men and we will go in."

"I would like to, Lieutenant, but we have a situation here with an entire village. Let that fellow walk ahead of you. They won't do anything to him. When things are under control, I'll send Officer Wanninger into the mill to help you."

I walked ahead of Lieutenant Brunn. As we crossed the field and neared the mill, I heard shots. I dared not turn around. I did not hear Brunn say anything. The firing lasted a long time, several minutes. I do not know if any Reserve Policeman took up the major's offer and refused to kill the villagers. If there were any who did, I do not know who they were because I had my back to the villagers and was walking toward the mill.

By this time I had managed to loosen my trouser belt. In the mill I overcame the lieutenant and strangled him. I stripped his uniform off and put it on. I took his revolver and put it in the holster. I disappeared from the field into the forest.

From the distance the Reserve Police major must have been sure I was Lieutenant Brunn. He waved to me. He did not seem to notice I was walking alone. I walked away from the mill, in the opposite direction from where the villagers had been assembled. I walked quickly. All I managed to see before I entered a small forest behind the mill was the major directing his soldiers. They seemed to be lifting bodies. The major did not seem to be interested in what had happened in the mill—maybe he did not want to question the judgment of a Gestapo lieutenant. Maybe he thought Brunn had machine-gunned the partisans.

Concerning the massacre at Klibiski: There are three names I can testify to: Lieutenant Brunn, Major Schnitke, Reserve Policeman Wanninger. The first did not participate in the massacre at Klibiski. I do not know what Reserve Policeman Wanninger did.

[signed:] Abraham Zeligman

4:00 pm Lidia Adler Orthopedic ward—room 414, Hadarim Hospital

I tiptoe in. Vera's alone. I suppose her parents have gone to talk to the nurse, and Baruch must be with Thomas. I sit on the very edge of Vera's bed and whisper in her ear, "I brought you something, *mi pequeñita* Vera."

She opens her eyes. "The photograph, me and the lilacs."

"They're for good luck. Remember, you said—a symbol of everything that's beautiful in life."

Since she's started to talk, she keeps asking me if she said anything when she was unconscious. I always answer, "Nothing." It's the truth, so why does she keep asking me?

I've watched her mother and father since they got here. They get along much better with each other than Vera said they did. Maybe when he left, and afterward, everything seemed worse than it really was. Some people are better off divorced.

She's closed her eyes. Even when Vera is sleeping, I talk to her. The idea is to keep the person connected, especially someone who's seen the terrible things Vera has. I heard someone in the hospital say that cameramen and reporters never show or describe what it really looks like—it's just too awful.

I take my camera, and I focus. "Forgive me, Vera," I whisper, and I shoot.

Someone squeezes me from behind. I turn around.

"Dan!" We hug each other.

"How are things going?"

"She's been sleeping on and off. The nurse gave her a pill for the pain about ten minutes ago."

"You want to get some coffee, Lidia?"

"I wouldn't mind," I say.

"Then I'll stay with her. Go ahead. Take your time. If you see her parents, tell them I'm with her and we want to be alone."

That's what I like about Dan. He says what he thinks and doesn't worry what people will say about it.

Before I go, there is something I want to tell him. "She's terrified of what she's going to look like."

"I know."

"She's scared stiff she'll be ugly, that there will be scars from the metal and glass, people will stare at her, no one will be able to love her. That you won't love her."

"She is the only person I love or will ever love."

"And you'll let her know it?"

"Every minute of every day, even with scars or crutches or double-thick eyeglasses."

"I love you, Dan, and so does she. See you later." I give Vera a quick squeeze on her good arm. She moves a bit, opens her eye, and smiles.

"I know I look like a pirate with this horrible patch," she says.

I quietly close the door. I see Vera's parents coming toward me, toward the room. I meet them at the elevator. "Dan's in the room with her. Do you want to have some coffee?"

They look at each other. Alex shrugs his shoulders. "Yes, of course, Lidia."

4:00 PM Thomas Wanninger Intensive care unit—Neurology, Hadarim Hospital

A few hours ago Mutti told me about Herr Ben Tov's past. I kept asking her, Will he come back here, to the hospital? She had no answer. How could Mutti have told someone? Someone here in Israel?

Mutti said she had no choice. Someone had to help us find out the truth. "But after he helps us, you will come home. There will be no need to stay in this violent place."

Yes, yes, home, I thought. Home safe with Mutti, and Christina, and my friends. It's too bad that I can't follow the plan, discover the truth about Opa by myself, but once I have an answer, I can go home and leave the old man in peace. Mutti is afraid. I'm all she has, so I've got to say it, don't I? "Yes, Mutti. I'll come home. Of course."

She looked down at her hands. "Thank you. I didn't imagine this would happen to you. I didn't imagine such horrible things were possible."

But what will I tell my uncle Friedrich—that I'm not a Jew lover anymore? And Christina, that my curly hair is not because I have Jewish blood?

"You're still very sick, Tommi. Anyway, it will be a while before you are even out of the hospital."

I said nothing. I can't tell Mutti yet what I saw on the ground next to me. In my worst dreams about Opa I never imagined anything like what I saw. I'll never forget.

"I am going down to the cafeteria to get something to eat." She leaned over to kiss me. I stared at the wall above her head.

I hear Dr. Stitti in the corridor. He is doing his afternoon rounds, checking the patients in the unit. Today they may move me out of ICU. I close my eyes. I am very tired. I hope I don't see any pictures in my mind. I want my head to be empty of everything that's terrible.

"Tommi?"

I turn my head. It is Herr Ben Tov.

"Herr Ben Tov, I don't have enough words to say how sorry I am. To ask you to do all that for me when you yourself have suffered so much," I say. "Please accept my apologies."

He takes my hands in his. He looks at me and then says the strangest thing. *"Nein, ich bin es, Tommi, der sich entschuldigen muss."* He is apologizing. To me.

Why is he saying he's sorry? He's done so much for us. I should ask his forgiveness. Now I know how bad a memory can be.

Dan Oron Orthopedic ward—room 414, Hadarim Hospital   4:30 PM

"Did you bring it?" she asks.

"I promised I would, didn't I?"

"Against your will you promised. That's why I thought you wouldn't."

"Yes, against my will because it's much too soon. It's a miracle you're alive."

"Don't get spiritual with me. Just take it out."

She is leaving me with no choice. That's one thing about Vera: Saying no to her is like banging your head against the wall. I unzip my backpack and take it out.

"Is that the most recent one?"

"Yes."

"Okay, let me see it."

I give her the photograph.

It's hard for her to hold, so I prop it up on the blankets, near her knees.

"It's awful, I'm awful, absolutely disgusting. Frightening. People will run away from me."

"You are in a hospital. You were in a bus explosion. Do you honestly think this is the way you will look for the rest of your life?"

"Yes."

"No. No, this *not* the way you will look for the rest of your life. It will take months until everything heals, your legs, your arm, the cuts, and your eye. Put the picture away and look at me."

"No."

"Yes, because I brought something else. Something much more important than a picture."

"What?"

"Your application."

She doesn't say anything. Just stares at the IV, at the EKG monitor, at everything that says she was injured, and at her photograph. I wait.

"Will it happen? Both of us, Dan? Together? Studying?"

"It will, I promise you it will."

"Help me sit up."

I prop the pillows up behind her back and press the button to raise the bed. I do it as gently as I can.

"Switch on the overhead lamp."

I take out a pen. "So, do I start filling in your application?"

"Yes," she says.

My hand is shaking a bit. "Name?"

"Vera Brodsky."

I start to write, and then I look up at her. She has got to be the most amazing person in the world.

"Why are you looking at me that way? Don't you believe I'll be well enough to study botany? Or maybe you think you're going to study archaeology on your own and find another girl-friend?" She laughs and then she cries.

I take a tissue and wipe away her tears. "I'm looking at you because there's no one in the world like you and I'll never have anyone else."

"And you'll never leave me?"

"You've been unconscious for too long. You don't know what you're saying." I kiss her gently. "I love you, Vera."

"Really and truly?"

"Yes."

"Will you stay with me? I want to tell you something."

"I'm not moving."

"I had a boyfriend in Odessa. His name was Sergei Rubinstein." She stops and looks at me.

I kiss her again. "Notice I'm still here."

"Pull the curtains around my bed," she whispers.

"But there's no one in the other bed," I say.

"I don't care, pull the curtains," she says.

I get up and pull the curtain. We are alone, no one can see us.

"He did something terrible," she says in a low voice.

I can barely hear her. "What did he do?"

"He killed himself, and . . ."

"And?"

"And maybe I'm to blame."

Of all the things that I thought Vera would say, I never expected this.

"Why would you think that?"

"Because I think I didn't love him enough."

"You are the most loving person I know. I can't live without you and I'm going to live and so are you. Both of us. Together. Do you hear me? Do you understand, you ridiculous botanist from Odessa? Is that why you've been so afraid to tell me we'll study together, live together?"

"Yes." It is a very quiet "yes."

"I'm sorry he died. But I'm not him. And I won't leave you. I won't do to myself what he did. Never, absolutely never."

She turns her head toward the narrow table near her bed. "Did you see the photo Lidia brought me—the lilacs?"

4:45 PM **Thomas Wanninger** Intensive care unit–Neurology, Hadarim Hospital

I remember the blackness, the pitch blackness, as if I were squeezed between two walls. No air, no light, my mouth moving but no words. My mouth was full of water that weighed like stones. Water like stones, stones like water. It made no sense. After that, nothing. Then pain, pain so great it swallowed me, and silence, white silence.

The first voice I heard was Opa Hans—he was talking to me about Israel and Jerusalem. I was dead and he and I were in Heaven. We were talking about holy places because we were in Heaven. Only later, much later, did I know it was Baruch Ben Tov.

Now he's here, in my room. Mutti is not here.

"I have something to read to you," he says. He opens an envelope and takes out a sheet of paper.

"'I was arrested on August 2 by the Gestapo. . . .'"

*   *   *

176

When he finishes, he asks me, "Does this help at all, Thomas?"

"I don't know. Who sent my father the photos, the same ones you saw? It must have been someone whose family was killed there. And why would they send it to my father and to Yad Vashem?"

"Maybe Wanninger, Otto, was the only name they found. Maybe it was not to blame, to point a finger, but to say 'Do something, do something in the name of your relative.'"

"So you think Opa didn't do it, he wasn't part of the massacre? So why did he run away? Disappear?"

The old man doesn't answer. He looks very tired.

"I'll never know for sure what really happened," I said.

"What happened belongs to another time and place. We will never know everything. We will never be able to really explain. You know much more than you did when you came. Be satisfied with that."

"I suppose you're right. After I get better, I am going home. My mother is very afraid for me. She wants me back in Berlin. After I tell her about Opa, she will certainly say there is no reason for me to stay."

He doesn't answer.

"Baruch, what do *you* think?"

"I think none of us can see into another person's heart. We can't understand what makes us do as we do, what makes us hate, what makes us love. A mother does everything she can for her child, and when she can't . . ."

He pauses for so long that I say, "And then?"

"Her heart breaks."

"Mutti has done everything for me."

"Yes, she has, Tommi."

"And I *should* go home with my mother, right? Leave here?"

He hesitates. "Yes, you should," he says.

5:00 PM Muhamed Abutayeh Sanur, Palestinian Authority

I have completed all the preparations. I have taken my oath on the Koran and in the name of Allah. My parents will receive the videocassette and the photograph. Anaam will have my photograph in front of the holy mosque in Jerusalem and the letter that is only for her eyes, my fiancée's eyes.

I pray she will be happy.

The car is a white station wagon, stolen last month, which can carry the four bombs, the three gas canisters with the inflammable liquid, and the three containers of nails, bolts, and other sharp metal objects.

The target has been picked. A place of celebration, a crowd of happy Jews, eating, dancing, singing. I have entered the enemy's territory many times. No one suspects me. My father will be able to buy farmland with the money he will receive from the *shaheed* fund. My death will be honorable.

I know exactly what to do. The time and date have been set. I will not fail.

6:25 PM Dr. Ibrahim Stitti 14 Khirbet Salih Street, Beit el E'Nab, Palestinian Authority

I have never been able to figure out why it takes women such a long time to get ready. "Nadine, we'll be late. We have the checkpoints to cross." No answer.

I'm in a good mood this evening. The German boy is out of his coma, and I'm almost willing to bet there will be no long-term effects. Of course, this is something I haven't told his mother. After all, there are no guarantees in life.

"Nadine, it's a bar mitzvah celebration. I promised Dr. Razine we wouldn't be late. Can't you hurry it up?" No answer, just the sound of the shower being turned on in the bathroom.

The children are with my mother. Peace and quiet. I turn on

the radio. The six-thirty news. Nothing, just the usual political nonsense, a garbage collector's strike, a famous tennis player gets defeated. Good, maybe the insanity of the suicide bombers has run its course.

The shower is turned off. "Nadine, how much more time do you need?"

"Ten minutes and I'll be ready," she answers in the sweetest voice imaginable. That's a woman for you.

FRIDAY, APRIL 14

Ilse Wanninger Waiting room, Hadarim Hospital   5:45 PM

Someone has lit two white Sabbath candles and placed them on the small table here in the waiting room. The Jewish Sabbath is beginning.

Tommi was awake for quite a few hours today. He is happier now that he is in a regular room. From his bed he can see the green hills. We talked about Opa Hans and Herr Ben Tov. We talked about killing, about hate, about being terrified, about having horrible memories. Then he slept a bit.

When he woke up, he asked me, "Do you think Opa was a killer, that he was part of the massacre?"

"I don't think so," I said.

"Then why did he disappear?"

"I don't know, Tommi. I've asked myself that a million times and so did your father. And probably so did Oma."

"Yes, but she would never answer my questions."

"You know, Tommi, whatever he did or didn't do, he found a solution to his dilemma. I feel that in my heart. Maybe he died, maybe he ran away, maybe he was shot."

"I'm glad I came here, Mutti, even with everything awful that's happened. I always thought every question had an answer. Like in an exam. Now—"

"And now you see that many questions have no answers." I kissed him. I looked at his face, the skin wounded, but also wounded inside. How long would it be until he forgot what he had seen? Until he wasn't afraid to go out, to travel, even in safe Berlin by bus?

"Baruch told me about his work, about the gardens, the planting," Tommi said. "Did you know that Vera has her own corner of a garden at the kibbutz, with a lilac bush? I could plant something too."

"I want you home, you know that."

"I know, Mutti. Maybe I'll come back someday."

He closed his eyes and in a moment he was asleep again.

Baruch has promised to take me to a church in Jerusalem on Sunday. I will thank God for giving Tommi back his life.

5:45 PM   Lidia Adler   Orthopedic ward—room 414, Hadarim Hospital

"*L'cha dodi, likrat kala p'nay Shabbat n'kabala.* It's me, Lidia, singing. Open your eyes. It's your favorite Sabbath song. Sing with me. Come on, pal, try, just a few words."

"*Shabbat shalom,* Lidia."

"And a peaceful Sabbath to you. I'm glad you're in a better mood. Nothing like taking a load off your shoulders and your heart."

"Are you mad I didn't tell you about Sergei?"

"How could I be mad at you? I just hope that one day you start trusting people. So welcome to this beautiful world."

"Is it beautiful?"

"Are you kidding? My best friend is alive—that makes it beautiful. For Dan too."

For a moment she doesn't say anything. Neither do I.

"He's sorry for me. Look at me. You should know—you keep taking my picture. And then I told him about Sergei. That made him pity me, not love me."

"Come on, cut it out. He's waiting outside, Vera. He loves you so much."

"I love him too," she says quietly.

"So?"

"So why would he want to live with a person who'll be afraid of the tiniest sound for the rest of her life? Who knows if I'll ever get out of here, be normal?"

"You're wrong. He knows you're really brave. You came alone to the kibbutz. You weren't afraid to start all over again after Sergei died. Hey, you're a Brodsky—your grandfather survived the gulag."

I say a tiny prayer in my head that she'll let Dan come in. That she'll start believing people won't leave her. I mean, if a prayer isn't answered on the Sabbath, then when?

"Okay, you're right," she finally says.

I open the door and give Dan the thumbs-up sign. He grins and comes in. From the doorway I take a picture of the two of them.

"I love happy endings," I say.

Sameh Laham, security prisoner 0593 Surgical ward— Isolation, Hadarim Hospital   5:45 PM

I hear the call to prayer from the muezzin. How clear the sound is. It comes through the half-open window of my room. The mosque is below, in the small village off the hospital road. Time to pray, time to pray.

I remember the words from the Koran for a *shaheed*. I remember the mother and baby. I do not turn in my bed to face Mecca. I do not pray.

5:45 PM **Baruch Ben Tov** Memorial grove, Kibbutz Broshim

Ilse phoned. Thomas was transferred from Intensive Care to a regular ward. He can see the hills from his window. He wants to know where the kibbutz is.

So much trimming and watering to do now that it is starting to get warm. Here in the grove the wind moves through the pine trees, like a mother smoothing a child's hair. Each tree is a memory of a life. Some trees bend one way, some another. And outside this green circle, life goes on.

6:00 PM **Thomas Wanninger** Surgical Ward A—room 301, Hadarim Hospital

My bed is near the window. Past the pine trees covering the hills I can see a road and cars moving. People going home, coming back from work, whatever. Quiet. Nothing exploding.

It's still light outside, but I don't know what time it is. I got my watch back—the strap is burned, the plastic is split into pieces. It stopped at 11:47. For the rest of my life I'll see the people on the bus: the driver humming while he gave Vera our tickets, the skinny guy behind me who coughed all the time, the baby in the pink blanket in the back crying.

At least I found out what I came to find out. Anyway, it's as much of an answer about Opa as I'm ever going to get. I'm not dreaming about trains and prisoners anymore. Dr. Stitti said I was a survivor.

I have the weirdest feeling that nothing bad will ever happen to me again. After all, almost being dead can happen to a person only once. Then you go on living—you do things, make plans. That's the way life is. At least I hope so.